PRAISE FOR
THE GRIM GRUESOME BOOKS

"amusing...dramatic...just the thing for...readers...who want Dahl-style jokes and adventure." - *The Times*

"a terrifying adventure...Grim is a truly villainous character.." - *Books for Keeps*

"All the frosty bearded splendour of the Norse sagas condensed into a fun, thrilling tale for kids with a taste for high adventure...tipped to be a best-selling series." - *www.waterstones.com (5-star Covent Garden bookseller review)*

"This series just keeps getting better and better! With plenty of historical detail thrown in, this is a well put together and wonderfully told romp." - *www.waterstones.com (4-star York bookseller review)*

"An outstanding novel, keeping you tense and on edge." - *Imogen, 10* "adventurous, exciting, action-packed!" - *Uji, 11* "gripping" - *Ben, 8*   "brilliant...I kept wanting to read the next chapter"- *Adam, 8*   "truly thrilling" - *Megan, 10*   *Members of York Children's Book Group*

"a corking yarn which is both fast and exciting."
- *Adele Geras*

"It races from page t

"Boys and girls will ch
despair and admiring their pluckiness. - www.

GRIM GRUESOME
VIKING VILLAIN

in

THE CURSED SWORD

ROSALIND KERVEN

www.grimgruesome.com

First published in the UK by Talking Stone 2008

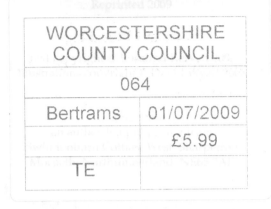

The moral right of Rosalind Kerven
to be identified as the author of this work
has been asserted in accordance with the
Copyright, Designs and Patents Act 1988

ISBN: 978-0-9537454-3-2

For David Fickling
who conjured Grim Gruesome out of the air:
magic helper extraordinaire!

A big thank you to my fantastic publishing team:
Editor: Helen Greathead
Designer: Alison Gadsby
Artist: David Wyatt

Collect the whole series of books about

GRIM GRUESOME
Viking Villain:

THE CURSED SWORD

THE QUEEN'S POISON

coming soon:
TROLL'S TREASURE

THE NORTH LANDS
A THOUSAND YEARS AGO
THE VIKING AGE

Come back through time to
the Viking Kingdom of Norway!

Away from the looming mountains
and the endless forests
was a bustling land
of farms and ships, towns and islands.
A wind blew over it from the grey North Sea,
smelling of salt and adventure.

1

Bjarni wasn't much older than you, but he had to work hard all day long, every day. He was a servant on a big farm. He looked after a herd of pigs for a rich, bossy farmer called Thorgill.

One midsummer's morning, Bjarni set out to take the pigs to graze in the oak wood. They scurried past the big, wooden farmhouse, oinking, squealing and grunting.

The farmhouse door creaked open and a deep, irritable voice yelled:

'SHUT UP!'

Then out stomped Thorgill, snorting into his beard. 'Keep those belly-wobbling beasts quiet!'

'Sorry, sir,' mumbled Bjarni.

'Sorry? I'll give you sorry!' Thorgill shouted. 'You

can't even look after the pigsty properly. I was down there last night and it stinks of giant farts! Get back there at once, you lazy oaf. Go and clean it out!'

Bjarni let the pigs into the wood then went grumpily back to the pigsty. He had to admit Thorgill was right: it was revolting. He started raking up the filthy straw, but the smell made him feel sick. So he rushed outside to get some fresh air...and stopped short in surprise.

A very peculiar man was standing in the yard.

This man was extraordinarily tall. Even though it was a warm summer's day, he was wrapped from head to foot in a thick cloak. He had the hood pulled right up so that his face was completely hidden. But Bjarni could feel the stranger staring at him.

'Quickly, Bjarni!' the stranger cried. 'Leave what you're doing. Get down to the road at once. You haven't got much time!'

'Who are you?' said Bjarni. 'What are you talking about?'

'Ach, throw away your questions!' said the stranger. 'Remember what Odin All-Father said: *The quick shall catch the prize.*'

'But I can't just leave my work,' said Bjarni. 'Farmer

Thorgill will go mad if I...'

'Wolf-spit!' the stranger whispered. He brought his hands out from under his cloak. They were enormous and hidden in a pair of thick leather gloves. He clapped them briskly, three times. Then he brushed past Bjarni and strode away.

A shiver ran down Bjarni's spine. He watched the gigantic man hurrying past the pigsty. As the stranger rounded the corner, his dark brown cloak seemed to melt into the wood. Bjarni blinked...and the stranger vanished!

Bjarni shrugged and went back to clearing out the straw. But he couldn't get the stranger's words out of his head. They nagged at him like a buzzing fly.

After a while, he couldn't stand it. He propped the rake up against the wall and glanced around to make sure that no one was watching him.

Then he ran towards the road.

2

This road was like all roads in the kingdom: it was just a dry, beaten mud track. On one side of it there were green fields full of corn and cows. But on the other side there was thick forest. This forest stretched away to the towering peaks of distant mountains shrouded in swirling mist.

The road was deserted. The summer's afternoon was hot and still. Birds twittered. Mosquitoes danced in the heat-haze.

Bjarni stood on the verge, hesitating. Why on earth had the hooded stranger sent him here? What was he supposed to do?

Suddenly a pony appeared on the horizon. It came trotting towards him. Bjarni squinted against the sun, trying to make out who was riding it. It looked like a girl...The pony drew closer. Yes, it *was* a girl...of about his own age. Suddenly he realised who it was. His heart began to pound.

Thor's thunderbolts, he thought, *of all people it's HER!*

It was Astrid - farmer Thorgill's daughter!

Astrid was really pretty. She had pale blonde hair and thick, dark eyelashes. She always wore brilliantly coloured dresses and aprons in the latest fashion, big strings of beads and jingling bracelets. All the servant girls on the farm longed to look like her. And all the servant boys - including Bjarni - were madly in love with her!

Bjarni broke out in a sweat and glanced down at his clothes. His tunic and trousers were both torn and stained with pig-mess.

I'm not letting her see me like this! he thought.

Quickly, he slipped into the forest. *I'll stay here until she's gone right past.*

And that would have been a good idea - except that somebody else was already hiding in the trees.

3

Astrid Thorgillsdaughter was on her way home from visiting her grandmother, who lived nearby on another farm.

Astrid's mother was dead. Her father was really strict. She had a stepmother called Gudrun, who was always putting her down.

But Grandmother was kind and funny. Grandmother spoilt her and gave her presents. Today she had opened her special ivory casket and given Astrid a whole bar of shining silver to add to her personal store of buried treasure.

Astrid had the silver bar in the little purse that dangled from her belt. She could feel it bumping against her leg as she rode along on her pony. She was daydreaming happily about the jewellery she would buy with it one day...

Suddenly a fierce voice came roaring out of nowhere:

'OI! YOU THERE! STOP!'

A vicious-looking man and a mangy dog burst out of the trees. Astrid screamed. It was a robber!

The dog went straight for Astrid's pony, yapping and nipping its legs. The pony neighed and reared up in fright.

'Help!' Astrid screamed. 'Save me! Somebody help me!'

She clung desperately to the pony's neck. Nobody came. The road was empty. Everything was lost! The robber would kill her!

He grabbed the pony's bridle and pointed a knife at Astrid.

'Get down!' he hissed.

Astrid slid from the saddle. She was shaking so much, she could hardly stand.

'Take off your beads and bracelets!' the robber snapped. 'Give them to me!' He prodded her purse. 'And what's in there, eh?' He felt it with dirty fingers. 'Feels like a bar of silver. Hand that over too, girlie!'

'No!' shrieked Astrid.

At that moment someone else burst out of the trees.

It was a boy in a torn shirt. He came racing towards them, dived to the ground, picked up a stone - and hurled it at the dog.

The dog yelped and jumped out of the way. The boy threw himself at the robber. He dragged the brute away from Astrid, stepped back, head-butted the robber in the groin and whacked his arm.

The robber groaned. The knife fell from his grasp. He swore and grabbed at the boy, but the boy fought back, wrestling, kicking and twisting away. He lashed into the robber, using fists, feet, knees, teeth, until the wretch was writhing on the ground.

'Get off me, you little rat!' the robber groaned.

Astrid could hear the boy's breath coming in fiery gasps. His dark hair was damp with sweat. His eyes were big with excitement.

Suddenly she realised who he was. He was one of her father's farm-hands - the dark-haired one who had been teasing her the other day with scary stories.

The boy glanced up at her. He was quite good looking. Astrid blushed.

'Are you all right?' he called.

'I...I think so.' She looked straight back at him and managed a shaky smile.

The boy - yes, it was Bjarni - hurled the robber's knife into a ditch. He gave the wretch a final kick in a place that made him scream with pain. The robber staggered to his feet, clutching himself. He spat at Bjarni and cursed him loudly. Then he called his dog and ran off, empty handed and limping, down the road.

4

'Thank you so much!' said Astrid. 'And thank goodness you were there! You were a real hero, leaping in to help me like that. What's your name?'

'Bjarni,' said the boy.

'I've seen you before,' said Astrid. 'You were pestering me and trying to frighten me. You're my father's pig-boy, aren't you?'

Bjarni nodded.

'Ugh!' said Astrid. 'Pigs stink. Keep away from me!' She wrinkled her nose. 'It's a pity you haven't got a sword to fight with.'

Of course, being just a servant, Bjarni couldn't afford to buy any weapons. But he was always practising with sticks and he knew he was good.

'I'll show you what I could do if I had one,' he said.

He clenched his fist as if he were holding a sword. Then he darted about, pretending to strike it into the air and stab it towards Astrid.

Astrid squealed and giggled.

The hooded stranger's words came buzzing back into Bjarni's head: '...*the quick shall catch the prize...*' He took a deep breath. 'By the way,' he said, 'I don't stink. Come here, and I'll prove it.'

He grabbed Astrid's hand. She pretended to push him off, but she was still giggling.

Bjarni took his chance. He pulled her close. She wriggled but didn't try to escape him. So he kissed her!

5

The next day, Astrid slipped out of the farmhouse and went to the oak wood, looking for Bjarni. Sure enough he was there, keeping an eye on the pigs. He was very pleased to see her. They started talking and got on really well.

After that, they met nearly every day. To tell the truth, they were besotted with each other. But they kept it secret.

'Think what people would say,' said Astrid, 'if they knew a rich girl like me was friendly with a raggedy servant like you!'

'I don't care,' said Bjarni. 'You know me. Nothing worries me. Nothing scares me either.'

'I bet some things do,' said Astrid.

'You're wrong,' said Bjarni. 'Try me with anything you want, and I'll prove it.'

'*Anything*?' said Astrid. 'Then...did you see that swarm of bees on the edge of the oak wood? There must be hundreds of them. If you're not scared of being stung to death by them, go and fetch me some of their honey.'

To her surprise, Bjarni nodded.

He scrabbled around on the ground and gathered up a bundle of twigs. He pulled out the little fire-making kit that dangled from his belt and struck the flint across the steel until it sparked and the twigs caught light. He let the flames die down until they were smoking, then set off for the tree where the swarm was.

Bzzzzz! The bees swarmed angrily around him!

But Bjarni didn't flinch. Boldly, he held up the smoking twigs. Soon the bees calmed down and settled quietly on the branches of the tree. Bjarni climbed past them, right up to their hive in the top branches and scooped a big piece of honeycomb out of it. He hardly got stung at all.

He gave the honeycomb to Astrid and watched proudly as she sucked the sweet honey from it.

'See,' said Bjarni, 'I can overcome any danger. I can do the impossible. Go on, ask me something else.'

Astrid tried to think of something she was sure he wouldn't be able to do. She said: 'Then...bring me some silver. But you mustn't *steal* it.'

Bjarni thought for a moment. Then he grinned. He took her hand and led her out of the wood to the banks of a wide river that flowed through the middle of the farm. He took off his boots and tunic, dived into the rushing water and disappeared below the surface.

Astrid screamed. 'Bjarni! Where are you? What are you doing? You'll drown!'

But a few moments later there he was - shouting her name from further along the bank. He stood there dripping wet, holding a big silver *fish* in his hand!

Astrid burst out laughing. 'Oh, Bjarni, you're brilliant!'

'Now what shall I do?' said Bjarni.

Astrid thought. She fiddled with her beads. She twirled her rings around her fingers. She smiled to herself.

He'll never dare do this! she thought.

'All right then,' she said. 'Go and ask my father if I can marry you!'

6

Astrid didn't believe for one moment that he would do it. But Bjarni didn't protest or argue. He shook himself dry in the sunshine and got dressed again. Then he ran straight off to the farmhouse.

The carved door was wide open, letting in the sunshine, so he marched straight in. He found Astrid's father, Farmer Thorgill, sitting on a bench by the fire in the big hall.

This hall was very grand and luxurious. The wooden walls were carved with twirling, interlaced lines and patterns. Colourfully embroidered pictures of the gods hung at either end. The wall-benches were covered with soft sheepskins. The high-seats were enormous and filled with silken cushions.

Thorgill was busy doing his favourite thing:

counting his silver. He was angry when he heard someone coming through the door to interrupt him. He was even angrier when he saw that it was Bjarni.

Bjarni marched boldly up to him. He bowed politely and said: 'Please sir, I've come to ask you something.'

'Whoah, there pig-boy!' cried Thorgill. 'What are you doing, barging in like this? Why aren't you working? Get back to your sty!'

'Ya sir, I will sir, I always take great care of your pigs sir. I'm only leaving them for a few moments sir.'

Thorgill glared at him. Bjarni hesitated. He almost ran straight out again. *But I can't let Astrid think I'm a coward!* he thought.

So he swallowed hard and blurted out: 'Please sir, can I marry Astrid when we're both old enough?'

'WHAT?!' roared Thorgill. He snorted loudly. His face turned purple. 'But you're only a servant! You come from a *family* of servants. You're always filthy and you stink of sweat. Your clothes are too small and all moth-eaten. How dare you think you might be good enough for a beautiful, well-bred girl like my precious daughter?'

He tossed a log into the fire-pit. Then he stood up and strode over to Bjarni. He was a full head and shoulders taller. 'You mangy weasel! This is an insult! You'd better be joking!'

Bjarni shook his head.

'I'm only twelve, sir,' he said, 'the same as Astrid. But by the time I'm sixteen I plan to have loads of silver saved up and eventually I hope to buy...'

'Don't make me laugh!' said Thorgill. 'I don't pay you enough to save anything. You don't seriously think I'm going to let my daughter marry a piece of rubbish like you, do you?'

'But Astrid loves me, sir!'

'So you've been pestering her, have you?' cried Thorgill. 'Threatening her, no doubt, until she says what you want.'

'I never...!'

'You creep! You could be fined for that, you know - you could be made an outlaw. I could kill you for it! Well, I can't have you working here any more, that's for sure. Get off my farm, pig-boy - by tomorrow morning!'

'But I haven't done anything wrong, sir,' cried Bjarni. 'I swear it!'

'Don't argue with me,' said Thorgill. 'And if I catch you coming back and bothering my Astrid again, you'll get a whipping!'

'But sir...'

'No, I'm not going to change my mind,' said Thorgill. 'Not for you or for anyone else. Get this into your fool's head: I've already found a husband for Astrid. It's an old friend of mine. His first wife died a few years ago, and he's got heaps of treasure stored away. He's already paid a really big bride-price to get betrothed to her. As soon as Astrid's sixteen, they're getting married.'

'But Astrid didn't say anything about this to me,' said Bjarni.

'I should think not,' said her father. 'She doesn't even know about it yet.'

7

Bjarni was in despair as he went out. But Farmer Thorgill was in a furious rage. He stormed straight into the side-room where Astrid's bony, sour-faced stepmother, Gudrun, was working at the weaving loom .

'Where's that girl?' roared Thorgill.

'Astrid?' said Gudrun. She had a thin, high-pitched voice like a rat's squeak. 'Well, I told her at breakfast she was to come and help me in here, but she's skiving as usual. What trouble's she making now?'

'She's brought shame on the family!' shouted Thorgill. 'I'm going to beat her black and blue! Get up woman - help me to catch her.'

Gudrun came at once, smirking nastily.

They both went stomping around the farm, looking

for Astrid. And where did they find her? By the pigsty of course, with Bjarni's arm around her. Bjarni had run straight back to tell her what her father had said. Astrid was crying and Bjarni was comforting her.

'ASTRID!' her father yelled at her.

Bjarni jumped and let go of her.

'It's not her fault, sir,' he said quickly. 'She was very upset and I was trying to...'

'GO!' Thorgill roared at him.

Bjarni threw Thorgill a dirty look and shook his head desperately at Astrid. Then he scuttled away.

Thorgill hurled a dry lump of pig dung after him. Then he turned to his daughter.

'You dirty girl!' he said. 'Fancy canoodling with a rough servant lad who hasn't a single piece of silver to his name! I'll be a laughing stock if anyone hears about this.'

'I don't care!' cried Astrid. 'And I'm not marrying some hideous old man that *you* choose for me, I'm not!'

Farmer Thorgill seized Astrid's shoulders and shook her. 'You ungrateful little fool!' he cried. 'What does it matter how old he is or what he looks like? There's only two things you need ask about a future husband, my girl. Number one: how rich is he?

Number two: do other people say good things about him? This friend of mine has a farm even bigger than ours. He's rolling in silver and everyone says he's very clever. I can assure you, he's the very best husband I could find for you.'

'But Bjarni's a free-born boy - he's not a slave,' said Astrid. 'He's going to work extra hard and save lots of silver - he's told me. So he'll be rich too when he grows up!'

'Just listen to her nonsense!' mocked Gudrun.

'He's so brave, Father. He saved me from a robber last month...'

'Oh, the silly stories and fibs!' said Gudrun.

'But it's true!' cried Astrid. 'He's a real hero. He's always doing things for me... I - love him!'

'Servants can't be heroes,' said Thorgill shortly. 'Now then, I'm telling you: forget that worthless boy.' He spat the words at her. 'Go and dry your eyes and wash your face. Then get back to helping your stepmother at the weaving loom like you're supposed to.'

'No!' cried Astrid.

Thorgill turned purple again. 'How dare you argue with me like a boy?' he shouted. 'Have respect for your father!' He slapped her hard across the cheek.

'I hate you!' Astrid shrieked.

Her cheek burned. Tears streamed down her face. She didn't even stop to think. She twisted away and went running off across the fields.

She ran and ran and ran. When she reached the fence that marked the edge of the farm, she hitched up her dress and climbed right over it.

On the other side, the road stretched off into the distance. Which way should she go? She couldn't think straight. So she threw herself down onto a boulder by the side of the forest, hid her face in her hands, and cried and cried.

Suddenly she heard the sound of hooves. She listened. Her heart missed a beat.

Oh Thor, save me! she thought. *Supposing it's another robber?* She looked up fearfully.

A huge man on a huge horse was galloping along the road towards her.

8

As soon as the horse reached her, it stopped. It was the most beautiful horse Astrid had ever seen.

It was much taller and sleeker than the farm ponies. Its coat was deep black. Its mane and tail were grey flecked with silver, very long and silky. It had big, dark eyes with silvery lashes even thicker than Astrid's.

The horse stared at her intently. Even through her tears, Astrid couldn't help looking back at it. The horse stepped closer. Its breath was hot on her face. Astrid reached out and stroked it.

Then she suddenly remembered there was a rider as well. She looked up at him nervously.

At first, all she could see were the folds of his long, dark-blue cloak, which seemed to go up and up for ever. Even when her eyes reached the top, she couldn't see the rider's face, because he wore the hood pulled right forward. The cloak was fastened with a silver brooch, shaped like a snarling wolf. His big hands were hidden in leather gloves.

'Astrid,' he said softly. His voice was friendly but it had a rough, gritty edge to it. She was sure she recognised it. She must do, she must have met him before if he knew her name. But she couldn't think who he was.

She jumped to her feet, and quickly tried to dry her tears on a corner of her apron.

'I'm glad you've made friends with Haski,' said the man, gesturing to the horse. 'But don't you remember your own uncle?' He laughed deeply in the back of his throat.

Astrid had quite a few uncles. But they all lived far away and she hadn't seen any of them for years. She shook her head.

Her uncle leaped down from his horse. His cloak blew wildly in the warm summer wind, giving off a faint smell of rotten meat. A sword gleamed underneath. In the shadows of the hood she could just make out a coarse, dark beard and deep-set, bloodshot eyes.

'You've been crying,' he said. 'What's the matter?'

'Nothing,' said Astrid quickly.

'Oh, come now,' he said, 'you can't be shy with your own uncle. Let me guess what's wrong. Is it love troubles? That's what pretty girls like you usually cry about. Tell me about it, Astrid. It'll make you feel better. I might even be able to help.'

He leaned back against the fence. Astrid peered up at him, trying to make out what he looked like under the hood. But then Haski started whinnying. He didn't stop until Astrid turned to look at *him* again. He nodded his silvery head up and down, up and down.

As she watched him, Astrid couldn't stop herself. She blurted out: 'I've just had a terrible argument with Father, because he found out about my boyfriend.'

Her uncle nodded. Haski nodded.

'He's called Bjarni,' said Astrid. 'He's really strong and really brave. I think I love him! He went to ask Father if we can get married one day, but Father refused and flew into a temper. He wouldn't even consider it. Bjarni's his servant, you see, and he hasn't got any silver at all. Now Father's sending him away - and I might never see him again! Then he's going to force me to marry some horrible old man instead!'

'Tut-tut,' said her uncle. 'And what's Bjarni going to do about this?'

'I don't know,' said Astrid. 'But he'll think of something. He always does. He has to!'

She started to cry again. Haski stamped and snorted.

'I have an idea of how Bjarni could get hold of some treasure,' said her uncle slowly. 'But it's rather...' His voice trailed off. 'No. No. It's unthinkable!'

'What is it?' cried Astrid.

'I feel sorry for you both,' said her uncle. 'But I mustn't give you dangerous ideas.'

'What ideas?' said Astrid.

Her uncle shook his head. 'Forget I said anything. Go home like a good girl, and make it up with your father. Then say goodbye to Bjarni. You'll get over it.'

'I won't!' cried Astrid. 'I don't want him to go!'

'Well,' said her uncle, 'he'd have to go off anyway for a while, even if...'

'If what? Tell me uncle!'

'You're very insistent, aren't you?' said her uncle. 'You're forcing me to make unsuitable suggestions. What I was going to say is this: Bjarni *could* get hold of enough silver to marry you - if he joined a pirate ship.'

Astrid stared at him in horror. 'Pirates?' she cried. 'I don't want my Bjarni going round with ruffians and murderers!'

'Exactly my dear,' said her uncle. 'As I said, it's unthinkable.'

He stooped. His face was still lost in the shadows of his hood, but now it was on a level with hers. The beard poking out was as black as Haski.

'I know you love jewellery and expensive clothes, Astrid,' he said, 'but you wouldn't feel comfortable if Bjarni started *stealing* things like that for you, would you? And that's what pirates do of course. And you'd feel just the same if Bjarni brought back enough silver to persuade your father to let him marry you. You'd turn it away if it was stolen - wouldn't you?'

'I'd hate Bjarni to be a pirate!' said Astrid. 'I've heard they're all dirty, drunken brutes. They beat people up. They *kill* people. They...'

'A nice girl like you doesn't want to be involved in that sort of business,' said her uncle soothingly. 'Let's forget it, eh?'

He let out a rattling laugh and swung himself back

onto the horse, leaning down to her.

'I have to go now,' he said.

He patted Haski and whispered in his ear. The horse began to walk slowly on down the road.

'Aren't you coming up to the farm, Uncle?' Astrid called, going after them.

Haski's silvery tail swung back and forth, back and forth. It gleamed and shimmered in the late afternoon sun. She couldn't take her eyes off it. She felt weak and slightly faint.

'Aren't you going to see Father?' she said.

'It's *you* I came to see, Astrid,' her uncle answered.

Haski broke into a gallop. Her uncle's cloak billowed out behind him. Astrid stared after him.

He reached a bend in the road, stopped and threw off his hood. But he had his back to her and he was a long way off. She still couldn't see what he looked like.

9

Astrid tried to sneak home without anyone noticing her. But Thorgill was still in a fury about Bjarni. He was waiting by the door to catch her and he gave her a hard whipping. Then Gudrun took great delight in sending her straight to bed without even a taste of supper.

Astrid lay in her bed-cupboard, tossing and turning for ages, thinking about pirates. When she fell asleep, ruffians and murderers didn't even enter her dreams. Instead they were lit by gleaming treasure hoards.

Midsummer nights in the North Lands are very short. Astrid woke up as soon as it began to get light. Everyone else was still sleeping. She got up and slipped out of the farmhouse.

She went to the hut where all the servants and

slaves slept and peeped through the door. Bjarni wasn't there. She went to the pigsty. Bjarni wasn't there. She climbed onto a tree-stump and gazed across the fields.

In the distance she saw a familiar figure. It was striding towards the farm gate with a bag slung over its shoulder.

'Bjarni!' Astrid cried, running after him. 'Wait!'

Bjarni spun round. He looked tense and just as miserable as her. He grabbed her and gave her a quick kiss. Then he said, 'Well, we'd better say goodbye.'

'*I'm* not saying goodbye,' said Astrid. 'Listen, Bjarni, there might be a way we could still get married one day after all!' She described the strange meeting with her uncle, and what he had said.

'Pirates!' said Bjarni. 'Oh ya, that's a brilliant idea! I should have thought of it myself. I tell you what: I'll go straight down to the town harbour now, and see if there's a pirate ship there I could join.'

'I knew that's what you'd say!' cried Astrid. She hugged him. 'You never let me down, Bjarni. You're so brave. I'll come with you.'

'Won't you get into more trouble with your father?' said Bjarni.

'I don't care,' said Astrid. 'I want to know what happens to you, Bjarni. I promise I won't get in the way. And I can take one of the ponies, so you won't have to walk. Just wait here.'

She ran to the stables, saddled a pony and galloped back to Bjarni. He jumped up behind her and they set off along the road.

By the time the sun was high, they had reached the town. It was a bustling maze of narrow lanes. It stood on the shores of a broad fjord - a stretch of water surrounded by mountains, that led out to the open sea.

The road gave way to a track that wound between many small, tightly-packed wooden houses. It was laid with planks and littered with rubbish. At the far end it opened onto the harbour. Bjarni and Astrid jumped down from the pony and tethered it to an iron ring set in a wall.

The harbour was a long curve of muddy sand, shaped like a horseshoe. It was really busy. Big baskets of fish and writhing lobsters blocked up the pebbly bank above it. Crowds of men and women were buying and selling things, gossiping and shouting. Gulls dived and shrieked. Boats and ships were constantly coming and going.

Bjarni and Astrid walked slowly round the harbour. Most of the boats hauled up on the sand were ordinary ones for fishing, ferrying passengers or carrying goods for trading. However, at the far end, bobbing up and down in shallow water, there stood a sinister-looking, black-tarred longship.

This ship had a hideous, grinning monster carved into the prow. It rocked and creaked on the water. Round, brightly painted shields were clipped along the sides, gleaming like a row of weird suns.

'I'm sure that's a pirate ship!' Bjarni whispered. 'Look, they're loading it up. It must be getting ready to go raiding!'

The pirate captain was standing on the beach by the ship. He was yelling at some men carrying barrels of drink and sacks of food aboard. He was an ugly looking fellow with jagged fighting scars all over his arms and face. But he wore loads of heavy silver arm-rings and neck-bands: his raids were obviously going well.

Astrid swallowed. 'Go on then,' she said.

Bjarni drew himself up tall and took a deep breath. Then he marched up to the captain.

'Get out the way, urchin,' the captain snarled at him.

'Can I join your crew?' said Bjarni.

The captain threw back his head and belched with laughter.

'By thunder, little laddy, what have *you* got to offer the great Captain Kvig?' he said. 'Are you any good at battering down church doors? Or slitting people's throats?'

'I'm strong and I can work really hard,' said Bjarni.

'Listen, you pimply skinny-pants,' bellowed Kvig, 'That's nothing to me. I don't have any work for little boys. I only take grown men - ones that are hungry for blood. If you want to join my crew, you'll have to sword-fight me first and prove you're a fearless, savage brute. I don't suppose a ragged little beggar like you has ever even *held* a sword eh? You probably haven't even got a knife to call your own! And - ha! - you look too small even to kill a fly.'

Bjarni flushed and turned away.

Astrid came running up to him. 'How did you get on?' she asked excitedly. 'Are you joining the ship? Tell me, Bjarni!'

Bjarni didn't answer. Instead he said quickly, 'Let's go over and look at the market. Maybe we could get something to eat.'

The market stalls were dotted around an open space above the middle of the harbour. It had started to rain, so there was hardly anyone around. They bought wooden cups of frothing beer and hunks of warm rye bread from a food hut. As they ate, they wandered past the other stalls.

Bjarni headed straight for one selling weapons. It had a large display of spears, axes, knives and swords.

'Oh come on!' said Astrid.

She tried to pull him over to another stall that was piled with gleaming jewellery, carved walrus-ivory combs and other pretty things. Bjarni ignored her.

The rain grew harder. Astrid sighed impatiently. They both hugged their cloaks tighter round them and pulled up their hoods. So did the stall-holder. He stood behind his display tables watching them. He was a very tall man with massively broad shoulders. His dark beard poked out over the top of his midnight-blue cloak. The cloak was fastened with a brooch like a snarling wolf.

Astrid felt a shiver run up her spine. She nudged Bjarni and tried more urgently to pull him away.

But nothing would keep Bjarni from a display of weapons.

The stall-holder called out, 'So, Astrid. We meet again.' The gritty voice was unmistakable.

10

'Uncle!' Astrid whispered.

'So this is Bjarni, is it?' said Astrid's uncle. 'Good morning, young man. Pleased to meet you.'

Bjarni looked up. When he saw Astrid's uncle, his heart missed a beat. Surely this was the hooded stranger he'd met just before he'd saved Astrid from the robber! His gigantic size was the same. His voice was the same. Only the cloak was a different colour.

'Good morning, sir,' he mumbled. He picked up a knife and put it down. He examined a spear.

Behind the stall, a huge black horse with a silvery mane stamped and snorted.

'Can I help you with something?' said Astrid's uncle. 'Would you like to buy something from my stall?' He sounded very friendly.

'I'm looking for a sword,' said Bjarni.

'Are you now?' said Astrid's uncle. 'Well, there's plenty here to choose from.'

He came out from behind his stall, towering over them in his dark cloak.

'The trouble is, I can't afford to buy one,' said Bjarni gloomily. 'I need a sword really urgently, but I haven't got any silver at all.' He turned suddenly to Astrid. 'You're rich though. Could *you* lend me some?'

'Oh!' Astrid looked startled. 'I don't know...No, I can't. I'm sorry Bjarni. Father takes all my treasure away - even what Grandmother gives me - and buries it in the forest. He won't tell me where it is until I'm sixteen.'

'But that gold band you always wear round your neck must be valuable,' said Bjarni. 'Or your rings - or bracelets - surely some of those would be enough?'

'Bjarni!' said Astrid's uncle sharply. 'You're trying to make Astrid give away the jewellery her poor dead mother left her. I'm surprised at you!'

Bjarni flushed.

Everything had gone very quiet. The only sound was the rain spattering steadily onto the sea.

Bjarni wandered along the stall. At the far end stood

a big table displaying a neat row of swords. They gleamed dully in the storm-light. Some were antiques with well-worn hilts and ominous stains on their blades. Some were brightly polished and brand new.

Bjarni looked at them carefully. He longed to hold one!

Astrid's uncle had his back turned. He was deep in conversation with Astrid.

Bjarni couldn't take his eyes off one sword in particular. It was a new one and beautifully made. The hilt was jet-black iron, decorated with twists of yellow gold, with a grip of soft black lambskin. The blade was covered in swirling patterns and lights that shifted and shimmered like waves on the sea.

He glanced up. Only the horse was watching him. It nodded its head and whinnied softly.

Bjarni reached out and touched the sword. Astrid's uncle still had his back to him.

Quickly he pulled the sword off the table. It was heavy, but the hilt fitted perfectly into his hand. The blade was so sharp that, when he turned it sideways, it seemed almost to disappear.

It was Bjarni's biggest dream to own a sword like that.

'PUT THAT DOWN!' Astrid's uncle yelled.

Bjarni jumped. Hastily he rammed the sword back onto the table.

Astrid's uncle came hurrying over. He grabbed Bjarni's arm and steered him away from the table. He wasn't wearing gloves today. His left hand was deformed. There was a stump where his little finger should have been. It looked disgusting: black, shrivelled and scabby.

'I should have warned you about that sword,' he said. 'Keep away from it, Bjarni. Don't touch it again.'

'Why not, sir?' said Bjarni.

For a moment Astrid's uncle didn't answer. The rain fell heavily. Then he said, 'That's no ordinary sword. I made it myself.'

'Is it really valuable, then?' asked Astrid.

'More than valuable,' he answered. 'It's priceless.'

'How do you mean, sir?' asked Bjarni.

'Have you ever heard of the sword owned by the god Freyr?' asked Astrid's uncle.

'I know that story!' said Bjarni. 'Freyr's sword was supposed to have the power to fight all by itself.'

'Exactly right,' said Astrid's uncle. 'And I've given *this* sword the same power.'

'Fight by itself?' said Astrid. 'But that's impossible, isn't it?'

'Is it?' said her uncle. He snorted. 'Well, I'm looking for a man brave enough to try it out for me. The sword isn't for sale, but I'm willing to lend it out for nothing to find out if it really works.'

'For nothing!' cried Bjarni. 'Oh sir, I'll try it...'

'No you won't,' said Astrid's uncle. 'Borrowing this sword is very dangerous. That's why everyone I've offered it to so far has refused to touch it.'

'Because it can fight by itself?' asked Bjarni.

'No,' said Astrid's uncle. 'It's because of the marks and runes. Look.'

He pointed to the black iron guard that crossed the hilt. A set of tiny, spiky lines and circles had been carved into it. Bjarni hadn't noticed them before. The shapes reminded him of animals and people, but they were very strange.

'These marks give the sword its power,' said Astrid's uncle.

He spun the sword over and pointed to the other side of the guard. There were lines carved on this side too. Bjarni recognised them at once as rune letters.

'Can you read runes?' Astrid's uncle asked them.

Bjarni and Astrid both shook their heads.

'No, I didn't think you could,' he said. 'Well, I'll tell you what they say. Listen.'

He traced the lines with the little finger on his good hand, reading them out slowly:

ᛋᛏᚩᛗ:ᚠᛁᚾᛏ:ᛈᛁ ᛏᚾᛁᚾᚠ:ᚦᚾᛏᛏᚱᚾᛋ:ᚾᛁᛏ
'STORM-WIND! LIGHTENING! THUNDEROUS NIGHT!

ᚠᛏᛏ:ᚦᛁᛋ:ᛋᛈᛏ:ᚻᛋᛋ:ᛒᚱᚾᚠᛏ:ᛁᛏᛋ:ᚤᛁᛏ
WHEN THIS SWORD HAS PROVED ITS MIGHT

ᛒᛏ:ᚠᛈᛆ:ᛁᛏ:ᚠᛁᚦ:ᛏᚱᛁᛋᛆ:ᚻᛈᛏ
PAY FOR IT WITH TREASURE HOARD

ᚠᛆ:ᛒᛏᛏ:ᛋᛏᛈ:ᛒᛏ:ᛈᛆ:ᚠᚱᛁᚤ:ᚱᛁᚠᛏ
OR PAIN SHALL BE YOUR GRIM REWARD

'You see, Bjarni, if I lend it to someone, he has to agree to the deal. If the sword works, he has to pay me with the treasure it wins for him. If he tries to cheat his way out of paying, I shall make him suffer for it!'

51

Suddenly he swung up his big, hairy hands and held them in front of Bjarni's face. They smelled overpoweringly of rancid fish and old sweat. The fists were clenched. The throbbing veins stood out like blue ropes. The stump of his missing finger oozed puss.

Bjarni flinched. But he said steadily, 'Supposing he genuinely *couldn't* pay you? Supposing...you know, it wasn't his fault, because he didn't have any treasure to start with, and even with the sword, he couldn't get hold of any?'

'I don't accept excuses,' said Astrid's uncle. His voice was so low, they could hardly hear him over the sound of the rain. 'Let me warn you, Bjarni: I have a very violent temper.'

Bjarni nodded.

'I won't frighten Astrid with the details,' her uncle went on, 'but I can assure you, by the time I'd finished, that man - that *cheat* - would wish he'd never tangled with me.'

'I...I understand,' said Bjarni. He thought for a moment. Then he nudged Astrid's arm, stepped aside and beckoned her to follow him.

'Did you hear all that?' he whispered. 'This sword could solve the whole problem! I don't have to worry about paying for it to start with - and if it's really as good as it's supposed to be, it could win me a place on the pirate ship!'

'But supposing it doesn't work?' Astrid whispered back. 'Supposing you take it and can't pay him when you're meant to, later on? You heard what he threatened! He'll...'

'Aw, come on!' said Bjarni. 'He's your *uncle*, Astrid! He's bound to make some allowance because of that. And how else can I get hold of a sword for nothing? I've got to have one, or the pirate captain won't even consider letting me join his ship. Don't worry, as soon as I get some treasure, I'll make sure I take some straight to your uncle. If the sword really works, I'm bound to have plenty left over too - for us! To persuade your father!'

'You're so brave,' Astrid told him.

Bjarni went back to the weapons stall.

'Sir,' he said to Astrid's uncle, 'Please could I try out your special sword? I understand the condition about paying for it with treasure eventually, and I fully accept it. I swear I won't let you down. You said you'll lend it out for nothing at first...?'

'I did,' said Astrid's uncle. 'But not to *you*, Bjarni.'

He laughed drily. 'I like you. I wouldn't enjoy punishing you if you broke our bargain.'

'I promise I won't break it sir,' said Bjarni. 'I swear I won't! I *have* to do this. It's the only way I can join the pirate ship and win some treasure, so I can marry Astrid. It's my only chance.'

'Are you refusing to listen to my advice?' said Astrid's uncle. 'Then you're an impetuous little fool, Bjarni.'

'No he's not!' cried Astrid. 'Why does everyone say nasty things about Bjarni? He's never scared of anything - he always does what he says - he's a hero. Can't you see that, Uncle? In Thor's name, Bjarni, take the sword! Show my uncle, show the world, what you can do with it!'

'Well Bjarni,' said Astrid's uncle, 'did you hear that? The lady herself has spoken. What passion! You'll have to do what she says. Ha! Let's seal the bargain.'

He reached under his cloak and unhooked the meat-knife that hung from his belt. He held it to the sword guard and quickly nicked some more tiny lines and hollows into the black iron.

'There,' he said, 'that says:

ᛅᚴᚱᛁᛏ:ᛒᛅ

‘AGREED BY

Then here’s your name...

ᛒᛅᚾᛁ

BJARNI

‘...and my name...’

ᚴᚱᛁᛘ

He scratched four more letters onto the guard. But he didn’t read them out. Instead he spat onto the runes, leaving a little puddle of green froth. He rubbed this carefully into the black iron with his finger-stump.

‘I’ve done what you asked for,’ he said. ‘It’s too late to change your mind.’

11

Astrid's uncle went over to another table. He rummaged through a pile of things lying on it and gave Bjarni a scabbard and a shoulder-belt. Then he handed him the sword.

Bjarni swallowed. He put on the shoulder-belt, clipped the scabbard to it and slipped the sword inside. It looked enormous.

He led Astrid away from the stall. It was still raining hard. He stopped in the shelter of a tall warehouse, pulled off his cloak and gave it to her to hold. The rain soaked into his shirt and plastered his hair to his head. He grinned bravely at Astrid, then walked briskly back to the longship.

Kvig sneered and guffawed when he saw him again.

But Bjarni said loudly, 'I've got myself a sword now. I've come to fight you, like you said. I've come to prove I'm good enough to join your crew.'

He drew the sword from its scabbard. His fingers tightened on the lambskin grip. It fitted perfectly into his hand. The new blade gleamed through the rain like a silvery fish flashing in water.

Kvig's expression changed.

'Odin's eye socket!' he swore. 'Where did you steal that from, urchin?'

Bjarni didn't answer. He was breathing heavily. He held the sword ready.

Kvig drew out his own sword. He lunged at Bjarni with a vicious roar.

Bjarni dodged him and swept the sword through the air. It arced down and smashed against the captain's blade in a resounding clash of metal. Kvig staggered back.

Bjarni was drenched in sweat. The spiky runes seemed alive under his fingers. The blade shimmered in the storm-light. The sword was perfect to hold, like an extension of his own hand. It seemed to weigh nothing, but his arm throbbed with its mysterious power.

Kvig came at him again. Bjarni was ready, and struck back. He moved incredibly fast, incredibly nimbly. The sword sliced through the air like lightning. He was here - then he was there. He darted about. He met each of Kvig's thrusts with even more daring ones of his own.

Astrid waited in the shadow of a hut. At first she was so afraid, she could hardly watch. But when Bjarni began to gain the upper hand, her heart soared and she crept nearer. She clutched his cloak and silently cheered him on.

Suddenly the captain hurled his own sword down.

'All right, all right, you little piece of scum!' he yelled. 'You're good. I *will* give you a trial place in my crew after all. And if you prove yourself when it comes to real fighting, I might even keep you on.'

'Ya! Oh ya!' Bjarni slid the sword neatly back into its scabbard and punched the air in triumph.

Astrid ran up, breathless with excitement, and tried to hug him. But Bjarni brushed her away. His eyes were shining - but not at her.

Astrid's stomach turned over. *What's the matter with him?* she thought. *He's never been cold like that to me before.* She remembered her uncle's warning about the sword and looked at it nervously.

But there was no time to say anything, for Bjarni was already hurrying down the beach and splashing through the sea shallows to the pirate ship. The sword hung proudly in its scabbard, swaying and bumping against his leg. He kept glancing down at it and patting the hilt.

He reached the ship and then leaped aboard as if he were a long-standing member of the crew. At once, Kvig picked up a horn and blew it loudly.

As its echoes died away, a crowd of rough, burly men burst from the town lanes and came swaggering and shouting across the sand. They swarmed on board and sat down on the cross-benches behind the shields. Bjarni looked like a midget amongst them.

Astrid stared helplessly at the ship. She waved at Bjarni...but he was so busy admiring his new weapon that he didn't even see her.

Astrid sighed. She turned away and glanced fearfully towards the weapons stall. To her surprise, all its tables were empty. Her uncle and his horse had disappeared.

12

Captain Kvig and his pirates didn't return until the autumn.

It was late afternoon. The sun was setting over the sea, red as blood. The puddles on the harbour road were slowly turning to ice. The harbour itself was almost deserted, with only one or two late fishermen still unloading their catches.

The black longship came speeding down the fjord with a great splashing of oars. Just before the beach, its crew jumped out and hauled it onto the sand with a loud bump.

Astrid was there, waiting for it. She'd been sneaking down here nearly every day for months, even though she was in bad trouble at home. She stood on tiptoe, looking for Bjarni.

The pirates were singing crude songs at the tops of their voices as they pulled out their bags...

There he is! Astrid thought.

Bjarni's hair had grown long and straggly and his clothes were more ragged than ever. But the leather bag he carried was bulging.

Astrid called out to him, raced down the sand and flung her arms around him.

Bjarni was dirty and smelly, covered in scabs and scars. Astrid clung to him. They walked up the beach and turned onto a narrow road lined with warehouses and stables. He squeezed her arm but he didn't say anything.

'What's the matter?' said Astrid. 'You're not ill, are you Bjarni, or wounded?'

'It's just...a bit strange to be back here,' said Bjarni, 'but I'm fine.'

'Thank goodness!' Astrid babbled. 'But what have you got in your bag? Has the captain paid you?' She reached out and patted it. It was full of hard shapes and it jangled softly. 'Is it...treasure?'

Before Bjarni could answer, another voice, gritty and deep, came at them like an echo:

'Treasure - ya, *my* treasure!'

Somewhere close by a horse snorted and stamped. Then a huge man strode out from behind a tumbledown warehouse. It was Astrid's uncle.

As usual he was wrapped in a dark cloak with a very deep hood. Under it, his sunken eyes glowed ominously red from the sunset.

'So, Bjarni,' he said, 'how was the sword I lent you? Did it work like it should?'

'It's really good sir,' Bjarni answered in a low voice.

'Ha! And did it win you plenty of treasure?'

'Quite a lot,' said Bjarni.

Astrid's uncle picked up a big leather sack that was lying on the ground behind him. 'Then hurry up and pay me,' he said.

Bjarni nodded. He opened his bag, reached into it and offered Astrid's uncle a handful of silver bars.

'I don't like jokes Bjarni,' said Astrid's uncle. 'Put those pathetic crumbs away and empty the whole lot into my sack.'

'The whole lot?' said Bjarni. 'But I thought I only had to *share* it with you...you know, give you half.'

'Wherever did you get that idea from?' said Astrid's uncle. 'You cheat!' He poked a long, black-gloved finger at Astrid. 'I didn't mention shares or halves to you, did I Astrid?'

'I...I don't know,' she whispered.

Her uncle turned to Bjarni. He said: 'You made a pledge to hand over *all* the treasure the sword wins.'

'But...but...' Bjarni's words came tumbling out. 'That's not fair! You never said...I didn't realise...I've got to keep *some* treasure for myself, sir - otherwise I'll never have a chance of marrying Astrid!'

'I'd better explain the deal you agreed to more clearly,' said Astrid's uncle coldly. 'Take out the sword and I'll show you.'

Reluctantly, Bjarni pulled the sword from its scabbard. Astrid saw that its blade was no longer shiny and clean, but covered in dark stains.

Astrid's uncle seized it from him. He turned it over so that the runes on the hilt were hidden. Now he pointed to the strange little lines and circles carved into this side of the guard - the marks that he had said gave the sword its power.

'You see these signs, Bjarni?' he said. 'Not many people know how to make them or read them. They're secret. They're magic. I learned them from a sorcerer. Ya! A real Lapp sorcerer. One who runs with the reindeer up in the wild tundra lands of the far north.'

Bjarni and Astrid each caught their breath. They had both heard strange stories about the Lapps. People who'd travelled to the far north and met them said they were savages. They had weird customs, their clothes were all made of furs and skins and they lived in tents instead of proper houses. They worshipped bears. And their sorcerers were said to be dangerous and cunning, experts in the darkest skills of magic.

Astrid whispered, 'What...what exactly do these signs mean?'

'They turn the runes into a *curse,*' her uncle answered.

'A curse?' cried Bjarni. 'What sort of curse?'

'It binds you to me like a slave, Bjarni,' said Astrid's uncle, 'a slave who brings me treasure. You must give me *all* your treasure - not just now, but month after month, year after year, for as long as you live.'

The red sun had set. The twilight had faded. It was completely dark. There was no one else around.

'But...you never explained this properly before!' said Bjarni. 'It's not my fault I didn't understand. Anyway, the sword you gave me...'

'*Lent* you!' snapped Astrid's uncle.

'...everyone I fight with it, I beat. I've never even

been wounded since I had it. It's fantastic - it's as if it were made specially for me. It can't be cursed!' He hesitated. 'I bet...I bet even *you* couldn't hurt me, now I've got the sword, sir! Why should I do as you say?'

'You're a fool, Bjarni!' cried Astrid's uncle. 'Don't you realise? The sword is already starting to control you. I can see it in your eyes. I can hear it in your voice. And as its power over you grows, so does the curse that binds you to me.'

In the darkness he pulled off his glove and snatched suddenly at a strand of Astrid's long hair.

She shrieked and tried to slip away, but he twisted the hair tightly round his scabby finger stump.

'You might think you can resist me with the cursed sword in your hand, Bjarni,' he said, 'but you are wrong. For if you try to break our deal, it's not you I shall punish - but *her!*'

'Uncle, what do you mean?' cried Astrid.

'*Uncle!*' he mocked her. 'You don't really think I have "family feelings" for you, do you, you pestilent child? Ach!' He spat loudly at her feet. 'All I feel for you - for both of you - is hatred and loathing!'

Astrid was shaking. 'But *why?* We haven't done anything wrong! We...'

'I'm really looking forward to the day that Bjarni breaks our bargain,' her uncle went on softly. 'For that will be the day that I come for you.' He stopped abruptly.

'Come for me?' Astrid whispered.

'You won't see me,' he said. 'You won't hear me. But you will *feel* my presence, Astrid. And then Bjarni and his sword will be totally useless, for there will be no escape.'

He bent down and came so close that only the darkness stopped Astrid from seeing into the hollows of his face.

'I shall steal away your sleep,' he hissed. 'Night after night, I shall force you to lie awake, Astrid. And as you lie there, trembling in the darkness, I shall show you evil things - horrible, bloody visions. After a whole month of sleeplessness, you'll start to go mad with tiredness. Then at last I'll let you drop off - but I'll fill your head with nightmares - with bones and worms and monsters.

'You'll fall into a cold, smelly sweat. Your face will turn grey and dry as ash. But I still won't be finished with you, oh no - not until I've turned your heart into stone - and crushed it up into worthless fragments of dust!'

Astrid began to cry.

'You'll end up a slavering wreck,' he went on. 'You'll look revolting. Bjarni won't love you any more. He won't even want to come near you. Just the sight of you will make him vomit!'

Bjarni slid the sword hastily back into its scabbard and started unclipping it from his shoulder-belt. He thrust it out at Astrid's uncle with trembling hands.

'Here,' he said hoarsely, 'you can have the sword back, sir.'

'No Bjarni,' said Astrid's uncle. 'Your name is carved into the hilt. You *have* to keep it.'

Bjarni swallowed. He glanced desperately at Astrid. 'Well then, all right. But...but you don't need to hurt Astrid. Please don't! I beg you! Of course I'll bring you all the treasure, I swear it! Only *please*, can't I keep just a *little* bit for myself? Otherwise I'll never be able to marry her!'

Astrid's uncle let go of her hair and thrust her away. She sobbed wretchedly.

'Are *you* daring to lay down the terms to *me*, you little wretch?' he growled at Bjarni. 'Don't you know yet who I am?'

'I...I don't know your actual name sir,' said Bjarni.

'I inscribed it on the hilt of the cursed sword, Bjarni. Let me show you.'

He snatched Bjarni's sword from its scabbard again, grabbed Bjarni's hand and forced his finger to trace the shape of the last four runes:

ᚠᚱᛁᚤ

'Listen, fools. I'll spell it out for you. G - R - I - M. My name is Grim.'

'But none of my uncles are called Grim,' cried Astrid. 'I'm sure they're not!

'Ach, let's stop pretending about uncles,' said Grim.

'Are you...Grim...?' said Bjarni hoarsely. He stopped and swallowed. 'Grim...*Gruesome?*'

Grim laughed so deeply it sounded like a drum rattling in the bowels of the earth. Then he snapped, 'Hurry up and hand over what you owe me.'

He held out his sack. The top gaped open like a mouth.

Bjarni groaned. Very slowly, he tipped the rest of his hard-earned treasure into it.

When he was done, Grim Gruesome picked up the bag and strode away into the shadows.

13

Oh Thor help us!' whispered Astrid. 'Is it *really* Grim Gruesome?! That brute you teased me about that time? I never realised...I thought you were making it up. Bjarni, what are we going to do?'

'I'd seen him before,' said Bjarni in a low voice 'just before I met you. He gave me the creeps. But when you said he was your uncle...'

I told him my secrets!' wailed Astrid. 'I trusted him! I feel sick just thinking...I never realised Grim Gruesome was real!'

Bjarni said, 'They say that if he gets you in his clutches it's impossible to escape.'

Astrid clung to him in the last of the twilight, sobbing.

'Couldn't you ask the men on your ship to help you beat him off?' she said.

Bjarni thought. 'They'd never believe me. They'd laugh me into the sea. Anyway, people say he's so cunning...They say no-one - not even the strongest warriors in the kingdom - can beat Grim Gruesome.'

'That can't be true! Surely...'

'It is! Look how he tricked us - he does that to everyone. That's why he's so dangerous. And there's no time: we're due to sail again first thing tomorrow.'

'You're not going away again so soon? Please don't!' cried Astrid. 'You've only just got back, Bjarni, I've hardly seen you. And supposing...supposing Grim Gruesome...' she shivered. 'Supposing he comes after me when you're not here? I'm so scared. I need you to protect me!'

'But I *am* protecting you,' said Bjarni. 'He said, he'll keep off you if I bring him more treasure. Well, I can't do that *and* stay with you, can I?'

He slipped the sword back into the scabbard and ran his fingers over the spiky runes and patterns carved into the black iron hilt.

'Don't keep touching it, Bjarni,' said Astrid. 'It's evil.'

'No it's not,' said Bjarni.

'How can you say that when it's trapped us...'

'Ya, I know all that. But even so, it's the most fantastic weapon, Astrid. You'd be so impressed if you could see me fighting with it.'

Suddenly he whipped the sword out and started slashing it through the air.

'Stop it!' Astrid screamed at him. 'Bjarni, I'm so scared of him...and now you're making me scared of you too. I don't know what...'

'BJARNI!'

Raucous voices were yelling his name from the town lanes.

'Where are you lad? Come and join in the fun!'

'Here come my mates from the ship,' said Bjarni. He swung the scabbard round on its shoulder-belt so that it hung more comfortably. 'I'd better go and find them. They'll have it in for me if I don't join in with their drinking and games.'

'Ugh!' cried Astrid. 'I knew they'd be ruffians.'

'At least they appreciate my skills with this sword.'

'Bjarni, you're not getting drunk all the time, are you?'

'Aw shut up!' he said. And ran off.

14

The autumn evening was completely dark by now. Astrid was the only person left by the harbour. Her heart was in her mouth. The shadows leaped out at her. An owl hooted. The water lapped against the wooden ships. Her head echoed with whispers of that deep, horribly familiar voice - the voice of Grim Gruesome.

'You're very insistent, aren't you?...

I have a very violent temper...

It's too late to change your mind...'

She felt her way tearfully through the darkness, back to the wall where her pony was tethered. Then she rode home.

Moonlight scudded eerily in and out of the clouds. In the forest, trees creaked, wolves howled and deadly spooks groaned. But worst of all was the curse, which hung like a dead weight around Astrid's neck. It sent her heart racing and tied her stomach into a tight knot. It was all she could think of.

When she arrived, she had another shock.

The farmyard was brilliant with torchlight. Horses and people were milling around and the carved oak door of the house stood wide open. Everyone was crowding in, talking excitedly.

Oh no, she thought wearily, *Father must be throwing one of his feasts.*

Astrid pushed past the chattering guests. Inside, under dozens of lamps, she saw a roaring fire and rows of tables piled with food and drink. Families from several neighbouring farms were already sitting down around them, all dressed up in their best clothes. Some of them spotted Astrid and waved at her cheerily.

Astrid forced herself to wave back. Then she turned and fled - and bumped straight into her stepmother, Gudrun.

'Astrid! Look where you're going!' she snapped. The false smile she'd been wearing for her guests quickly turned into a scowl. 'And where have you been sneaking off to all this time, instead of helping me, you wicked girl?' She stepped back. 'Look what a mess you're in, you're dirtier than a slave. Thank the gods you're not my real daughter - I'd be ashamed of you. Go and get cleaned up at once. Your father will have fifty fits if you appear like this in front of our special visitor.'

'What visitor?' said Astrid.

'You'll see soon enough,' said Gudrun.

Astrid turned away. Tears brimmed up in her eyes again.

'Astrid, my favourite princess!' said a kindly voice. 'What's the matter?'

Astrid turned round. It was Grandmother! She was all plump and beaming with her greying-blonde hair swept up into an extravagant style of plaits and curls. Her large bosom was resplendent in a smart, wine-coloured dress with big silver brooches.

Astrid hugged her and tried to swallow her tears. 'Grandmother! What are you doing here?'

Grandmother never normally came to their house. She'd kept well away, ever since Astrid's mother had died and Thorgill had got married again, to Gudrun. Grandmother and Gudrun couldn't stand each other.

'Don't look so gloomy, Astrid,' she said. 'You love feasts!'

'I do but...'

'Well, why aren't you all dressed up for it? I know: you've been waiting for me to help you! Come on then princess, let's go and find some things to make you look as magnificent as me!'

'I don't really feel...'

'Nonsense!' said Grandmother. 'You can't let me down after I've swallowed my pride to be here.' She put her mouth to Astrid's ear. 'Your father actually lowered himself to invite me tonight,' she whispered. 'He's got someone very important coming to dinner.'

'Who?' said Astrid.

Grandmother winked. 'He's invited all the neighbours, and he thought there might be nasty gossip if he left me out. I was in two minds whether to come, but I can never miss the chance to see *you*.'

'But who is this important person?' begged Astrid.

'We're in for an interesting evening,' said Grandmother. 'It's a fortune teller.'

15

Grandmother called out to one of Thorgill's slaves to bring them a basin of water and a soft linen drying-cloth. Then she took Astrid's hand and led her firmly through the crowded hall to the weaving room behind it. Astrid's chest of clothes and jewellery was kept in a corner of this room, behind the door. Astrid opened the lid with her own key and rummaged inside it.

'You've been crying over that servant boy again, haven't you?' said Grandmother, shaking her head as she watched. 'Listen, princess, you've got to get over him. I know he's an excellent lad and perhaps he'll even prove himself one day. But your father's right: a girl like you simply *can't* marry a servant.'

Astrid bit her lip. 'Grandmother,' she said, 'I'm so worried! You see...'

'Don't tell me now, my love. We can't do with worrying when there's a delicious feast waiting to be eaten - and an evening of entertainment to follow.'

'But something terrible happened today...!'

The slave came in with the water.

'Now come on,' said Grandmother. 'Give your face and hands a good wash, then choose what you want to wear. Save these terrible things to tell me tomorrow.'

Soon Astrid was clean and smart in her best blue dress and embroidered apron, fastened with her favourite bronze brooches. Grandmother combed Astrid's hair until it shone and helped her on with several sparkling bracelets and strings of beads. At the same time, she told a stream of silly, gossipy stories so that Astrid couldn't help smiling.

They hurried back into the hall together. Everyone was talking in low, excited voices.

Grandmother and Astrid found a space at one of the tables and sat down. Gudrun was sitting preening herself at the top table. Normally she would be in one of the high-seats beside Thorgill, but tonight they were both empty.

Grandmother nudged Astrid. 'Look how smug and hoity-toity your stepmother is tonight!' she whispered.

'Anyone would think she was the Queen of Norway! But you and I know that her back teeth are all rotten and under that expensive silk headscarf her hair's crawling with lice!'

Astrid giggled.

A horse neighed loudly outside. Everyone craned their necks towards the door. Astrid's father Thorgill walked in, very smart in his best tunic, baggy trousers and high boots. Behind him came the fortune teller.

Astrid had never seen a real fortune teller before. This one was a tiny woman, nearly as short as a dwarf. Her skin was so pale it was almost transparent, her eyes were watery and bloodshot, and her hair was so fair it was almost white.

She peered around quizzically at the waiting guests, blinking each time she passed under a lamp. Farmer Thorgill led her to the high-seats. She sat down and shrugged off her riding cloak. Everyone's eyes were on her.

Her dress and headscarf were both as black as midnight. Her apron was scarlet, trimmed with snow-white embroidered ribbons. Her brooches and strings of beads were polished black jet. She wore a pure white fox fur round her neck with the head still attached.

'Welcome one and all!' cried Thorgill. 'My friends, eat and drink in honour of our guest!'

Everyone began to tuck into the feast. There was roast beef, wild elk steaks, goose, shrimps and salmon. There was sweet bramble-and-bilberry soup, nut cakes, cloudberry jelly, thick cream and lots of beer. Astrid was starving. She ate until she could hardly move. Deep inside, she still ached for Bjarni. But in the warm, cheerful hall, Grim Gruesome and the curse on the sword seemed to be nothing more than a bad dream.

At last everyone was sitting back, loosening their belts and burping. Thorgill banged his cup on the table until the noise stopped. The fortune teller stood up to speak.

She looked like a little girl against the grand, towering pillars of the high-seats, but her voice rang out clearly.

'I can't begin yet,' she said. 'This hall's too bright. I only want nine lamps burning.'

Thorgill sent a servant to put out the other lamps. A hush fell on the spooky gloom. The fire flickered, casting eerie shadows.

The fortune teller said: 'Now I need some ladies to help.'

Several women came forward. The fortune teller set them to stand in a circle around her. She chanted a strange, high pitched song with words like a foreign language, and made the women repeat it in chorus, over and over again.

'Why are they singing?' Astrid whispered to Grandmother.

'Sshh,' she answered. 'They're calling up the spirits.'

The women went back to their seats. The fortune teller brought out a set of silver charms, holding them up for everyone to see. Each was carved like a different goddess or god. They gleamed in the dim light. She laid them out on the table in front of her, then leaned over them, cocking her head to one side.

'What's she doing, Grandmother?'

'Oh do hush Astrid! She's listening to things that no one else can hear.'

Everyone leaned forward in excitement.

Suddenly the fortune teller began to talk, very fast. First she described some unfortunate things that would soon happen. Everyone groaned and sighed. Then she talked about lots of good things. Everyone cheered and clapped.

'Thank you,' said the fortune teller. 'Now, before I

go, is there anyone who needs my advice?'

A murmur ran round the hall.

'Well,' said the fortune teller, 'I believe Thorgill has a quiet room where you can come and talk to me in private. I'll have time for everyone who wants to see me.'

Astrid jumped up, suddenly desperate. 'I've got to talk to her, Grandmother!'

Everyone else was standing up too. Astrid pushed her way through them to the high-seats. But Thorgill was already leading the fortune teller away and through the side door that led into the dairy.

People began to line up eagerly outside the dairy door. Astrid went to the front of the queue.

'Hey!' Gudrun grabbed her arm and pulled her aside. 'Get out of the way, with your disgusting manners!'

'But I want to talk to the fortune teller,' said Astrid.

'What! After you've stayed out all day and shamed your family? Certainly not!' sneered Gudrun. 'The only fortune you need to know is that you're going to marry the man your father's chosen for you!'

Grandmother put her hand on the stepmother's arm. She looked majestic next to Gudrun, who was skinny and slightly stooped, even in her best yellow party dress.

'Pigs' bottoms to you, Gudrun!' said Grandmother. 'Why don't you leave the poor girl alone for a change? Anyway, hasn't it occurred to you that perhaps the fortune teller will frighten her into behaving better?'

Gudrun looked down her nose at Grandmother. 'She's had plenty enough whippings to do that,' she said sourly. 'I don't need your foul-mouthed advice, thank you very much!'

Grandmother flushed and looked as if she might slap Gudrun. But just then Thorgill came out of the dairy and the fortune teller peered through the door at the waiting queue. She looked at Gudrun. She looked at Grandmother. Then her watery eyes fell on Astrid.

'You look as if you've got problems, lassie,' she said softly. She touched Astrid's arm. 'Make sure you come and talk to me later.'

Then she beckoned the woman at the front of the queue into the dairy. The door shut behind them.

16

Each person stayed with the fortune teller for ages. Some of them came out grinning. Some came out looking worried and pale.

At last it was Astrid's turn. She opened the door and went in. It was cold and dim inside the dairy. There was no fire. The only light came from a small table where a single lamp was burning. The silver god-charms were laid out beside it.

The fortune teller was sitting on a stool between the table and the milk churns. Her scarlet apron was spread neatly across her knees and her pale hands were resting on her lap.

'Sit down, sit down,' she said. 'You're Astrid Thorgillsdaughter, aren't you?'

'Ya.' Astrid perched awkwardly on another stool and stared at the floor.

'So,' said the fortune teller, 'your father told me you're driving him to despair, Astrid. What's the matter?'

The lamp smoked in the draught.

As Astrid watched it, the horror of Grim Gruesome and the curse came flooding back into her mind. Her stomach clenched. She bit her lip and shrugged.

The fortune teller looked at her sharply for a moment. She leaned across to the table and stroked the charms. Then she closed her eyes, chanted softly, cocked her head and put her hand behind her ear.

At last she said: 'I hear the spirits' whispers. They see the evil that is troubling you. They say it is possible to overcome it. But *you* must fight it yourself, Astrid.'

'Fight it?' cried Astrid. 'I can't do that! I'm not a boy! I wouldn't even know what to do.'

'Not all fighting is done with weapons,' said the fortune teller. She lowered her voice.

'There's something - some kind of evil object? - that you're really afraid of, is that right?'

'The cursed sword!' cried Astrid - and at once clapped her hand over her mouth and bit her tongue.

I shouldn't have said it, she thought. *Supposing Grim Gruesome finds out I've been giving away his secrets?*

The fortune teller said: 'A sword, is it? Well, you must seize it, Astrid - and fling it into the sea.'

Astrid shook her head. 'I can't. Bjarni...he's got it. He'll never let me even touch it.'

The fortune teller closed her eyes again and rocked gently from side to side.

'The spirits have revealed a second way to me,' she said. 'Tell me Astrid: who gave this thing its evil power?'

Astrid remembered the weird symbols engraved on the hilt of the sword; she heard Grim Gruesome's voice saying: *'I learned them from a real Lapp sorcerer...up in the wild tundra lands of the far north'.*

'A sorcerer,' she whispered.

'That must surely be the one they mean,' said the fortune teller softly, as if she were talking to herself. To Astrid she said, 'Go to him.'

'But he's up in Lapland,' cried Astrid, 'hundreds of miles away! How will I get there? How can I find him?'

'I don't know,' said the fortune teller. 'But you must. And when you find him, you must beg him to remove the evil power from the sword.'

'It's impossible!' said Astrid desperately.

The fortune teller sat very still, listening to the silence. In the flickering lamplight, tears dribbled down her bone-white cheeks.

'The spirits tell me a third way,' she said. 'Someone else - not the sorcerer - forced this cursed sword on you and Bjarni, didn't they?'

A picture of Grim Gruesome swam before Astrid's eyes, huge and faceless in the murky shadows of his hood. She shuddered and slowly nodded.

'Who?' said the fortune teller.

'I'm too scared to tell you!'

'Well, that doesn't matter. Just don't wait helplessly for him to hunt you down, Astrid. You must go back to him of your own free will...And you must give him something...I see it...something that you cannot bear to give. The spirits say...ya, that may break the curse.'

'But he's so awful,' cried Astrid, 'I couldn't possibly...'

The fortune teller took her hand and squeezed it in a grip which was light and dry as a bird's claw. 'You're not a feeble weakling Astrid, are you?' she said. 'Of course not. You must be able to do one of those things. Look, take this.'

She scooped the god-charms from the table and into her lap. The silver gleamed on her scarlet apron. She sifted through them and picked out one shaped like a hammer.

'Here,' she said, 'you need this Thor's-hammer more than I do. Wear it round your neck, Astrid, and may the great god protect you and bring you luck.'

She pressed the charm into Astrid's hand.

17

While Astrid was brooding on what the fortune teller had said, Bjarni was already miles away on the longship, heaving at his oar. The pirates were heading south on the rough open sea and it was pelting down with rain. The long, narrow ship was completely open, with nowhere to shelter. So Bjarni was soaked to the skin with rain, sea spray and sweat.

Sixty-four pirates were sitting in pairs on the rowing benches, one beefy man on each side, down the whole length of the ship. Above them a huge, blue-black sail billowed in the blustery wind.

Their swords, axes and shields were all neatly stacked along the side of the ship. But Bjarni wasn't fool enough to leave the cursed sword there. Oh no, he wasn't going to risk losing it, or someone stealing it!

He kept it safely in its scabbard under his rowing bench, with his feet resting firmly on top.

As they rowed, the pirates in front were bellowing out a raunchy song about wine and ravishing women. The rest were having a disgusting conversation:

'...remember that monastery where we sliced open the fat abbot's stomach?'

'Aw! And when we pulled out his guts, they were all greasy and popping open...'

'...ya, and then we hacked his legs off...'

'... screamed like a screech-owl when I rammed my sword in...'

'Ah-ha-ha!'

'Come on, Bjarni, what's the matter? It's your turn to tell us something juicy!'

The talk was making Bjarni feel sick. He clenched his oar and tried desperately to think of a tale gory enough to match the others. But before he could come up with anything, the man on the bench in front of him turned round, grinning with black, gappy teeth.

'Look at him!' he sneered, 'he's gone all pale...'

'You're like a woman, Bjarni!'

'Na, a new-born baby!'

They all roared with laughter.

'Dwarf spit, Kvig!' someone called to the captain. 'Why did you lumber us with this pathetic piece of rubbish?'

Kvig was standing at the back, working the rudder and chewing on a piece of dried meat. He snorted and licked a globule of fat off his moustache, watching Bjarni through narrowed eyes.

'Let him be,' he called.

But Black Teeth ignored him. He poked Bjarni in the ribs. 'You'll never be able to grow a beard, little boy,' he said, 'if you're scared of blood.'

'Lovely red, gooey stuff!' someone shouted.

'And why are you always huddling over that sword of yours?' Black Teeth went on. 'You're like a scrappy dog guarding a bone!'

'Woof, woof!' someone shouted.

'Come on doggie, lick my bum!'

'Yap, yap!'

Bjarni felt hot. Shame and fury bubbled up inside him like steam inside a sealed cooking pot. He tensed his foot inside his boot and rubbed it along the scabbard. He felt the cursed sword's power surge up into him.

Black Teeth rested his oar and climbed backwards

over his rowing bench. He spat at Bjarni. Then he gave the cursed sword a hard kick.

The sword slid sideways.

'Get off!' Bjarni roared. He dropped his own oar, grabbed the sword hilt, drew the blade clean from the scabbard and leaped to his feet.

The other men barked some more and roared with laughter:

'Baby's jealous of his toy!'

Bjarni leaped onto the bench, brandishing the cursed sword. All around the longship, the grey sea swelled and churned.

The sword seemed to vibrate in his hand. It was the same every time he held it. Energy flooded his body. The shadow of Grim Gruesome flashed before his eyes.

The sword was light as a feather. His arm was as strong as iron. He closed his eyes and lunged at Black Teeth. Blindly, he felt the blade pierce the other man's flesh.

There was a thud. Someone grabbed Bjarni's shoulders and shook him. They yanked his empty hand up behind his back. They kicked him hard in the back of the knees. The ship rocked violently.

'Leave it, Bjarni!' came Captain Kvig's voice.

Bjarni opened his eyes. Black Teeth was lying on the deck, cursing. Another man was kneeling by him, swabbing blood that oozed from his shoulder.

Bjarni was surrounded by a menacing circle of men. Kvig stood right in front of him. His big muscles quavered and pulsed. His silver arm-rings rattled.

'Put it away, Bjarni,' he growled.

Bjarni sat down heavily on his bench. He dropped the sword onto the deck and clamped his feet on top of it.

'You can't let him get away with this, Kvig!' yelled one of the men.

'I won't,' said Kvig ominously. 'Bjarni, very soon you and I are going to have a little talk about that sword of yours.'

18

As you know, Farmer Thorgill's house was big and luxurious as well as showy, with several small rooms leading off the main hall. Even better, the family didn't have to sleep on the wall-benches round the fire, like most people did. For there were two proper box-beds built into cupboards at the end furthest from the door. The big one was for Thorgill and Gudrun, and the small one was for Astrid.

Astrid's bed-cupboard was very cosy. There were hooks on the wooden walls, hung with ornate hair-combs, dried flowers and precious trinkets. She had a big pile of soft woollen blankets and bear furs, so she was always nice and warm.

Usually she loved pulling the little carved door tightly shut behind her. But this particular night was different. As soon as she got inside the bed-cupboard, she felt hemmed in. And even under her warm covers, the darkness made her shiver.

For something had crept inside with her. Something dirty and horrible was clinging to her.

It was Grim Gruesome's curse.

The curse was swimming in her blood. It was clamped inside her head, tight and sharp as a limpet. It took over her thoughts and filled them with ugly anger.

That fortune teller was rubbish, thought Astrid. *Her suggestions weren't any help at all - they were just ridiculous. And fancy saying I have to sort everything out myself! It's Bjarni who should be doing all that. He's the boy. He's the one who can fight. He's supposed to look after me.*

The curse was a massive stone, crushing and splintering her heart.

Not that it's any good relying on him any more. He didn't seem at all pleased to see me. I bet he secretly couldn't care less what Grim Gruesome might do to me. Perhaps Grandmother's right: I should try and 'get over' him.

She lay down, pulled the blankets and furs up to her chin and tried to go to sleep.

But Grandmother doesn't understand! I wish she'd let me tell her what happened, but she wouldn't listen. Anyway, I can't just forget about Bjarni, even if I wanted to - because if I don't keep a check on what he's up to, Grim Gruesome will get me!

The echo of Grim's mocking voice came slithering into her head. She put her hands over her ears, but she couldn't block it out. She tossed and turned until she was all hot and sweaty. She threw off the covers - and turned icy cold.

The curse twisted its tentacles further into her. Dim, horrible visions crept from the edge of the darkness.

'...Bones and worms and monsters'.

A scream rose in Astrid's throat. She crammed her fist into her mouth to stop it - fumbled clumsily with the door - flung it open - and leaned out.

In the middle of the hall she could see the banked-up fire glowing comfortingly. The curse seemed to shrivel a little in its light.

But if I don't at least try some of the things the fortune teller said, thought Astrid bleakly, *what else can I do? And how will we ever escape?*

The thought crept into her mind that they might *never* escape. Her mouth went dry. She swallowed and sat up straight.

But which one? They're all so difficult! Go back to Grim Gruesome? That's ridiculous! And there can't be any chance of snatching the cursed sword from Bjarni when he's not even here. So that just leaves trying to find the sorcerer... Well...I suppose it wouldn't be impossible to catch a ship to Lapland.

She tried to imagine it.

Aw, but Father won't let me have my treasure for another three-and-a-half years, so how will I pay my fare? And even if I could, all the sailors would probably refuse to take me - they'd say I'm too young to be travelling on my own. It's not fair! Everything's so difficult! What am I going to do?

She bit her thumbnail, hard, right down to the quick.

I suppose I could sneak onto a ship and hide...But I've never sailed anywhere before...Supposing I'm seasick? And what am I supposed to do when I get to Lapland? They say it's just a wilderness, so how will I find the sorcerer?

She was wearing the fortune teller's hammer charm on a silver chain, and she clutched it tightly. *Thor, please help me! I don't know if I dare!*

19

A few days later, Astrid wrapped herself in her warmest cloak because she'd heard it was already snowing up in Lapland. She made sure the Thor's-hammer charm was securely fastened round her neck. Then she rode to town, left her pony in some stables and wandered along the beach, looking at the ships.

The sailors were all busy loading and unloading trading goods.

'Where are you going?' she called out to them.

'We're off to Denmark,' one crew told her.

'Just along the coast,' said some others.

'England.'

'West-over-sea, right across to Iceland for the last trip before the winter.'

'Out past the islands to catch whales.'

'Orkney.'

'Round to Sweden.'

And then at last, 'Up north to Lapland.'

Astrid's heart missed a beat. She looked at the ship carefully. She mustn't forget which one it was. Then she wandered away into the narrow town lanes, trying to act as if she had nothing special to do.

Dogs and pigs came sniffing up to her. Geese followed her. Boys whistled at her.

She soon threw them all off. But she couldn't throw off Grim Gruesome's mocking voice, which kept echoing through her mind.

The autumn sun set early and the air turned cold. As darkness fell, she went back to the harbour. Everyone else was hurrying away home.

She longed to go home too. Instead she went up to the Lapland ship.

It was quite small: only as long as nine men lying head to toe along the quayside, and as wide as two. It curved up at either end like a swan's neck. The mast towered over the centre, with a rolled-up yellow sail at the top and thick ropes stretching down to the sides. There were three rowing benches. The deck between them was packed with barrels, boxes and bundles.

The tide was coming in. The far side of the ship was already adrift in the water. It was moored to an iron post in the sand: its ropes strained and creaked.

Astrid glanced around. The beach was deserted. Waves were lapping gently against the front of the ship. She leaned out and grabbed the side.

Trembling, she hitched up her dress. She swung a leg over and tumbled down onto the deck.

She had never been on board any kind of ship before. She was surprised at how shallow it was. Standing on the deck, the sides only came up to her waist. It would be easy to fall overboard and drown.

She clambered gingerly over the rowing benches, stumbling and slipping on the stuff crammed between them.

She found some barrels smelling of dried meat, cheese and beer. Her mouth watered, but the barrel tops were held down by heavy clips. Further along she came to a big heap covered by a grubby tarpaulin. She glanced round, then lifted up a corner of it.

Underneath were four fat bales of new woollen cloth, neatly stacked in two piles. The sailors must be taking it to sell up in Lapland. The cloth felt soft and warm.

She squatted down, held up the edge of the tarpaulin and wriggled under it. It was darker than night, like a cave.

She shifted the bales around into a hollow and crawled into it. There was just enough room for her to lie down. It was quite cosy. She loosened an end of cloth and pulled it over herself like a blanket. She curled up so that her feet weren't sticking out. She shifted the tarpaulin back over the top.

She was completely hidden, except for a small breathing hole near her face.

The incoming tide rocked the ship up and down. *Slip-slap* it went against the sides, *slip-slap*. It was very soothing. It even blocked out the nagging echo of Grim Gruesome.

Soon she was fast asleep.

She slept long and deep and peacefully. She didn't wake until the next day.

By then, the ship had been sailing for hours.

It had left the harbour far behind and was heading north. Now it was in calm seas, threading its way slowly between some islands.

20

Astrid peeped out of the tarpaulin. She must have slept for ages. It was daylight, but the sun was already sinking low again, staining the sky with gold and crimson. The yellow sail fluttered loosely in the wind. Six men were sitting on the rowing benches, heaving at the oars. Another man stood in the stern, steering with the rudder.

As she watched, the ship turned towards land and hauled up on a sandy beach. The sailors jumped ashore and began to unload things.

First came two sets of criss-cross tent poles, then big cow-hides to drape over them. Next came a black cooking cauldron. Finally they opened one of the barrels and pulled out some bags of food. They carried everything up the beach to a stretch of grass in front of a forest.

As soon as they had gone, Astrid crawled stiffly out of her hiding place. She slipped over the side of the ship and crouched down to pee behind it. Just as she stood up, one of the sailors came hurrying back - and spotted her.

'Mighty Thor!' he shouted. He ran towards her. 'Where did you spring from?'

Astrid backed away. 'I wasn't doing any harm,' she said breathlessly. 'Please help me!'

The sailor stared at her. 'We'll see what Captain Orm thinks,' he said.

He grabbed her arm and hauled her up to the campsite. The tent was already up and a fire was smoking away with the cauldron bubbling over it. It smelled deliciously of stewing meat.

'Look at this!' called the sailor, 'I've found a little beggar-girl hiding in the ship!'

The crew crowded round, staring at her.

'What's going on?' cried the captain. 'You wicked girl! What do you want of us?'

'I'm not a beggar,' said Astrid. 'I just want to come up to Lapland with you.'

'Are you crazy?' said Captain Orm. 'It's already winter in Lapland. The rivers are frozen, the snow's deep and the wolves are hungry. Look at you in your skimpy dress with its fancy trimmings! And that cloak! It might be the latest fashion, but you need double furs up there to keep you warm. How do you think you'll survive?'

'Well, sir, *you'll* survive up there, won't you?' she answered.

'You cheeky hussy!' said Orm. 'We have proper clothes to keep us warm and valuable goods to sell to make it worth the hardship. What do you think you're going to do when you get up there, eh? Go to a feast?'

Astrid said, 'I have to find a Lapp sorcerer.'

Captain Orm spluttered. 'A Lapp sorcerer! Whoever in Thor's name gave you that crazy idea?'

'It was a fortune teller,' said Astrid.

'A fortune teller!' cried Orm. 'What, one of those devious women who go round persuading fools to pay them a pile of silver for their made-up prophesies? I bet she never told you how deathly cold the winter is up in Lapland, eh? And did she teach you to speak the Lappish language? - because no one up there understands a word of Norse. And I hope she mentioned that the magic these Lapp sorcerers practise involves the most dangerous and evil kind of spirits!'

103

Astrid's stomach turned over. 'But the fortune teller said her advice would save me!'

'Save you from *what?*' said Orm.

Tears welled in Astrid's eyes.

'Look, I can see you're probably just an innocent and foolish girl,' the captain said more kindly. 'I feel a bit sorry for you. Why don't you tell us what's made you so upset, eh? Sit down. Have a bite to eat with us.'

Astrid felt much better, sitting round their fire and sharing their stew. The sailors were quite friendly. Surely they would help her?

After the meal, Captain Orm asked her again: 'Go on then. Tell us about this danger you're in.'

Astrid explained all about her and Bjarni, and how he'd got hold of a sword which turned out to have a terrible curse.

'So who gave Bjarni the sword?' said Orm. 'Who put the curse on it?'

Astrid didn't answer.

'She's spinning such a tale - next she'll be claiming it's Grim Gruesome!' said one of the sailors.

The others all guffawed.

Astrid caught her breath sharply.

'Aw, don't worry lass,' said the sailor, 'I was only

joking. That ruffian isn't...'

'But it is,' whispered Astrid. 'It *is* Grim Gruesome!'

They all stared at her in astonishment.

Orm said, 'That's just the way he works.'

The sailors exchanged looks and shook their heads.

'If he's got his claws into you, no wonder you're in a state, girl,' said Captain Orm. 'He's the most evil man in all the North Lands!'

The sailors began to discuss Grim Gruesome in low voices, constantly glancing over their shoulders:

'But isn't he meant to be out of the way in Sweden?'

'Ya, and our king ordered the border soldiers to keep him out of Norway.'

'What use are soldiers against Grim Gruesome? He'll have come here by the eagle route, straight over the mountains. They say that he and that horse of his...'

'Haski, it's called. It's said to be a beautiful creature...'

'Haski? That means "danger", doesn't it?'

'Exactly. The horse is supposed to be as cunning as he is. Anyway, they don't bother with sticking to paths...He goes anywhere he wants...'

'Have you heard how he forces people to put him up for the night? They say his threats are terrible!'

'Oh please listen!' cried Astrid. 'The fortune teller said a Lapp sorcerer could show me how to escape from Grim Gruesome. *Please* take me up north so I can find one!'

'Don't you realise, girl?' said Orm. 'No child can escape once Grim Gruesome gets his claws in them.'

The other sailors all nodded.

'Of course we all feel sorry for you,' said the captain.

The other sailors grunted their agreement.

'We'd like to help you,' said Orm, 'but...' He avoided Astrid's eyes and stared into the fire. 'We don't want to get ourselves tangled up with the brute as well. We've all got wives and children at home: we have to put them first. Grim Gruesome has spies everywhere. If you stay on our ship, he'll end up pouncing on us too - and that'll just make things worse for everyone, won't it? So I'm sorry, but we can't take you any further, girl.'

'But...what shall I do then?' said Astrid. 'I don't even know where I am. If I can't go up to Lapland, how will I get home?'

The sailors all shrugged. Captain Orm shook his head.

'Please,' cried Astrid, 'don't leave me here in the middle of nowhere!'

21

On the very same night that Astrid smuggled herself aboard Captain Orm's ship, Bjarni was staggering around a strange, exotic-looking building full of noise and people. It was nice and warm in there, with a big fire burning away in an ornate iron fire-pit; but the air stank of wood-smoke, beer and vomit. His head was swimming and he couldn't stop laughing.

Where am I? he thought. *Oh ya, I remember: this is a drinking hall. We're somewhere foreign where they all talk gobbledegook - France or somewhere.*

He had a fit of hiccups.

Fantastic raid today! What a load of treasure we got. And all those pathetic locals - I can't believe how easy it was to swat them down!

Captain Kvig came swaggering up, brandishing the

special drinking horn he always wore at his belt. It was a beauty, a polished pure-white ox horn, with delicate twists of shiny silver round the edge.

'Oh-hoh, Bjarni!' he cried. 'Enjoying yourself, lad? You farting well ought to be, seeing as half the treasure we're stacking up is thanks to you and that sword of yours. Take your reward, my friend. Have a swig from the hero's horn!'

Bjarni put the horn to his lips and spluttered as a stream of warm, spicy wine gushed into his mouth. As Kvig snatched it back from him, the room swayed... and Bjarni fell off his stool.

He lay on the dirty floor, feeling stupidly happy. Talk and laughter swished lazily around him like the summer sea.

Dwarf spit, he thought, *it's crowded in here!*

He staggered to his feet - and suddenly remembered the cursed sword. He patted his scabbard hastily.

Phew, still safely there.

He fingered the hilt, enjoying the familiar scratchy feel of the runes and markings.

You're all mine now, he thought. *My lovely Blood Drinker, that's what you are. All those battles we've fought together... surely Grim Gruesome hasn't got power over you any more? Why should I worry about his stupid curse?*

Bjarni went stumbling and grinning round the tables. He saw two of the pirates playing a heated game of insults, rolling up their sleeves for a fight. He saw Black Teeth tickling a pretty foreign woman who was sitting on his lap. He saw Kvig again, standing in a corner. He was rubbing his silver arm-rings, watching him.

Bjarni pulled out his sword and waved it at the captain. Kvig nodded and waved back with both arms. Bjarni glowed.

He let out a satisfying burp and sicked up the wine he'd just drunk.

Good job Astrid isn't here, he thought.

He sidled away from the mess and squatted on the floor. Then he lay right down and yawned.

Mind you, it's a pity she didn't hear old Kvig calling me a hero! That'd impress her.

The hilt of the sword was digging into his ribs, so he unclipped the scabbard from the shoulder-belt to get more comfortable and laid it carefully beside him. He wriggled out of the way under a table, rolled over onto his side and closed his eyes.

Dreams drifted through his mind: heaps of gold, the flash of his sword, people screaming as they fled before him...and then an enormous, faceless figure in a hooded cloak loomed ominously up. For a moment, an icy shiver went through him, but he was too tired to bother with it. Instead he curled up and fell fast asleep.

22

Sleep didn't come so easily to poor Astrid. She spent a horrible night on the island, worrying and shivering under a pile of grubby sheepskins in a cold corner of the sailors' tent. In the morning Captain Orm let her have a few scoops of their sour barley-porridge for breakfast. Then he took her arm and steered her firmly towards the forest behind their camp.

'Look girl,' he said gruffly, 'you go down that path through the forest. There'll be a farm on the other side. Ask the people who live on it to help you. But in mighty Thor's name, don't be fool enough to tell them about Grim Gruesome!'

He gave Astrid a hard shove. Then he hurried down to the beach, wiping his hands on his trousers, as if just touching her had contaminated him.

His men were launching the ship. As soon as Orm jumped aboard, they began to row away from the shore really fast.

Astrid stared after them in dismay. *They're really going to leave me here,* she thought. *The brutes!*

'Come back!' she screamed, 'come back!' But the ship gathered even more speed, rounded a headland and disappeared.

Slowly Astrid walked down to the beach and sank onto the sand. She was completely, utterly alone.

It's that stupid fortune teller's fault, she thought. *She made me do this. I thought it was impossible - and I was right. I bet it's true what Captain Orm said about her: she made it all up. So there's no point trying to do those other things she said either.*

The air was very still. The waves broke and broke. Their rhythm echoed and nagged at her:

Month-after-month.

Year-after-year.

As-long-as-you-live.

That was what it meant to be cursed.

She felt dirty and marked. She felt weak and dizzy. Bile rose in her throat. She spat it out and pressed her head down between her knees.

Something cold slithered up her chest and tumbled out of the top of her cloak. It was the Thor's-hammer pendant that the fortune teller had given her.

If she was any good, at least her Thor's-hammer would help me, but even that's probably useless.

Astrid clutched it fiercely.

Go on, protect me, bring me luck, prove the fortune teller's genuine!

The edges of the pendant pressed painfully into her palm.

'Thor,' she screamed out loud, 'please save me!'

Nothing happened.

After a while she sighed and stood up. The sea was covered in swirling mist. She gazed up at the forest. The trees crowded together, tall and sinister: sharp-needled pines and ghostly silver birch, stretching away into a tangle of darkness.

There'll be wild beasts in there! she thought, *and more robbers. I'm not going anywhere near it, I can't!*

Instead, she began to walk blindly across the sand.

The little bay ended in a wide expanse of rocks. She started to clamber over them. Their sharp ridges pressed painfully through her skimpy shoes. She slithered over crevices and patches of slimy seaweed.

Her woollen stockings tore and she scraped her ankle raw. On the far side she dropped down onto another beach.

She stood there miserably, hugging her cloak around her. A bank of heavy clouds filled the sky. The air was turning icy. It began to drizzle.

The drizzle turned to sleet. Her fingers and toes were numb with cold.

She ran on the spot to get some feeling in them, then sprinted down to the water's edge. The tide was going out, leaving the sand so wet it almost swallowed her up. She changed direction quickly and ran towards another lonely rock.

As she got closer, she stopped. It wasn't a rock after all.

It was a small boat.

Her heart missed a beat. *How did that get here?* She clutched the Thor's-Hammer. *Maybe he heard my prayers after all.*

'Thank you Thor!' she cried out loud.

The boat was was very old and storm battered. The rowing bench was split in two and the top of one side was a mess of splinters. There were no oars.

She leaned over and patted her hands carefully

across the bottom. She couldn't find any holes in it.

She gave the boat a hard push. It didn't move. It was too deeply embedded in the sand.

She squatted down and scrabbled with her bare hands. At last it came free. It slid suddenly down the wet beach and into the fast ebbing water.

Astrid raced after it, grabbed it and threw herself inside. She didn't have time to change her mind...

For at once the power of the tide and its mysterious currents took control and carried her quickly away. They spun her round and round, then swept her, through the fjord, right out to the open sea.

23

When Bjarni woke up, he wasn't in the drinking hall any more, but in the pirates' big camping tent. Bright daylight was filtering through the half-open door flap. All the other sleeping sacks were empty. There was no sign of the other men.

It must be tomorrow already, he thought. *But what time?*

His head throbbed badly. He felt jelly-legged and queasy. He couldn't remember going to bed. He couldn't remember last night at all.

He sat up carefully and slid out of his sleeping sack. *Ouch!* He saw his shoulder-belt and scabbard lying neatly beside it. Someone must have put them there. He reached inside the scabbard for his usual check on the cursed sword.

It wasn't there.

Bjarni leaped to his feet in panic. He banged his head on a wooden tent-pole and fell down again.

Someone's stolen it!

He crawled round the tent, frantically looking for the sword. He tipped out all the empty sleeping sacks. He scrabbled through the other pirates' mess of cloaks and stolen trinkets. Nothing. There was no sign of the cursed sword anywhere.

Grim Gruesome will go mad if he finds out!

He burst outside, blinking at the bright light.

'Where's my sword?' he yelled. 'Who's stolen it?'

The tent was pitched next to two others on a rocky promontory above a white, sandy beach. The other pirates were all lying around bare-chested in the warm, southern sunshine. Some of them shrugged. Most ignored him.

Bjarni staggered to a stream bubbling down the rocks to the sea, and splashed cold water onto his face.

A voice behind him called: 'Bjarni, my young friend! A word with you.'

He spun round. Captain Kvig was standing there, scratching an old scar on his nose.

He beckoned Bjarni away from the camp. They walked briskly to a clump of thorn bushes. There Kvig grabbed Bjarni's head and jerked it down to make him stare at the roots. Sticking out from the bottom was the rune-carved hilt of the cursed sword.

'Hey! How did it get there?'

Bjarni squatted down unsteadily and tried to grab it. But Kvig kicked his hand away with his big, sealskin boot.

'What is it about this wonderful sword of yours?' he said softly. 'What do those rune words mean? What are the strange markings for? Are they something to do with the power that gets into you when you fight with it? A power that seems to be...' He lowered his voice. 'How shall we put it...supernatural?'

'Let me have it!' cried Bjarni.

Kvig grabbed both his arms and yanked them up behind his back.

'You're not so strong without it, are you Bjarni? And yet when I hold it, I can't get any sense of the power for myself at all. Where did you get it from? How do you make it work?'

'I don't know! Just give it to me!'

'Not unless you agree to help me in return.'

'But I can't!' cried Bjarni. 'It's not properly mine. I've only borrowed it...'

'Who from?'

119

'I...I can't tell you. But I'll get into terrible trouble if...'

'Bull turds! Either I keep this sword myself, or you use it to help me force the other men back under my control. I'm sick of them all, answering me back and challenging my orders. Next time that happens, Bjarni, this is an order: stick your sword into the swine that's cheeking me, like you did with old Black Teeth out at sea. I want to see them grovelling!'

Frantically Bjarni tried to think back: *What did Grim Gruesome say about the curse? The sword has power over me because it's got my name on it, I know that...But can I use it for anything apart from getting treasure for Grim? Supposing he found out I'd been helping Kvig with it - would he do those terrible things to Astrid?*

His brain was all fogged up with stale beer.

But if I don't agree, Kvig won't give me the sword back at all - and when Grim discovers that, he'll probably torture Astrid and kill me!

'What's the problem, Bjarni?' said Kvig. He cleared his throat and smoothed his voice to a friendly tone. 'You ought to use this sword to get the maximum advantage, lad. So here's an offer: if you fight for me with it, I'll pay you double shares of treasure over everyone else.'

That would double the treasure I give to Grim, thought Bjarni. *If I give him so much...maybe it would soften him a bit. Maybe...* He shook his head hopelessly and gazed desperately under the thorn bush.

Kvig's boot nudged the sword a little further in.

'I'll make you my second-in-command,' said Kvig. 'That'll impress your rich little girlfriend!'

Bjarni felt himself blush. He imagined himself telling Astrid that he'd already been promoted to a high position in the pirate crew.

Kvig poked him in the ribs. 'Ya, and if you've got any sense, you'll start using the sword to get control over her too.'

Bjarni rubbed his aching forehead. 'I... I'm not sure,' he said. 'That's not how...'

'Of course you're sure!' said Kvig. 'Only a fool would own a sword like this and not use it to double his riches and win a high-class girl for his wife.' He seized Bjarni's hand and pumped it up and down. 'Good man! I knew I'd be able to persuade you. Here's your sword back.'

He pulled it out from the roots, wiped the muddy blade clean on his tunic and handed it to Bjarni with a flourish.

'Don't lose it again, Bjarni. I need it now as much as you do. Come on, let's go and put the fear of Odin into my crew straight away!'

24

A few days later, a burly fisherman came walking out of town and along the road that led to Thorgill's farm. He was leading a grey pony and a small cart. There was something alive inside the cart. It was wrapped in thick blankets and shivering.

Suddenly the cart was forced to stop. The road was blocked by a crowd of farm servants carrying axes, ropes and scythes. In the middle of them stood Thorgill and Gudrun. They both looked very agitated. Gudrun was twirling her bony fingers round and round the flappy ends of her headscarf. Thorgill was bossily shouting out instructions.

'You, you and you lot, go into the forest - hack through it if you have to - and search every track you see - even deer and elk tracks. The rest of you, work your way across the fields and search the river bank especially thoroughly. If you see any signs of her clothes, you're to dive in and search underwater...'

'Looking for someone, are you?' called the fisherman.

'It's my daughter,' said Thorgill, 'my precious Astrid, the prettiest girl in the kingdom. She's gone missing!'

'She's not by any chance a blonde-haired lass, about twelve or thirteen years old, is she?' said the fisherman. 'Because I so happen to have a girl of that description here in my cart.'

Thorgill rushed over and pulled back the blankets. Astrid's white, trembling face gazed out at him, wide eyed. As soon as he saw her, his tone changed.

'What in Thor's name are you doing, riding in that dirty fish box, you wicked girl?' he yelled. 'Your stepmother's right, all you bring the family is shame!'

Gudrun nodded vigorously.

'Now hold on,' said the fisherman. He was a kindly man with three daughters of his own. 'Last night me and my mate rescued her right out of the sea, poor thing. It seems someone had set her adrift in a boat, and she was very close to drowning.'

'Ya, and I know who did it for sure!' cried Thorgill. 'It'll be that wretched servant boy I chucked out. You've been sneaking out to meet him, haven't you, Astrid? Even though I banished him from the farm and forbade him to come near you ever again. Just wait till we get you home. I'll give you such a whipping...!'

The fisherman scratched his head awkwardly. 'Well, I hope there won't be any trouble,' he said. 'Now my friend, if you just help me out with her, then I can be on my way. I have to take this cart back to town, and I need to be out fishing with the evening tide.'

He looked at Thorgill expectantly.

'What are you hanging about for?' stormed Thorgill. 'You're not demanding a reward for rescuing her, are you? If you had any decency, you'd have done it out of the goodness of your heart, but I know what your sort is like. Well, I'm not made of treasure, you know, and I haven't got any silver with me right now. You'll have to come up to the farmhouse another time if you want paying. Now Astrid, stop acting sick and get out of that filthy cart.'

Very slowly, Astrid pulled herself upright. She looked dirty, battered and half starved. 'I don't want to come home,' she said weakly. 'I don't want to be whipped!'

The fisherman tutted.

Thorgill signalled to two of his servants. They leaned over the cart and grabbed Astrid's arms, one on each side.

'Leave me!' she screamed. In desperation, she twisted her head round, first one way and then the other, and bit both men on the hand.

Thorgill turned purple. He marched up to the cart and slapped Astrid really hard. Astrid shrieked. The fisherman looked away, embarrassed.

Suddenly a calm, husky woman's voice burst in on them: 'Whatever are you doing, Thorgill?'

It was Grandmother!

'Astrid, my little princess, what's happened to you? Thanks be to Thor that you're safe!' She turned to Thorgill. 'She needs looking after, not punishing. Get out of the way at once, you foolish man!'

She poked a plump finger in Thorgill's chest, and kept it there until he stepped back. His cheeks were puffing in and out with rage. Grandmother leaned over the cart and hugged Astrid into her large, soft bosom. Then she turned to the fisherman and said,

'Could you kindly bring her up to *my* farmhouse, good man? It's just up that path there.'

She pointed up the hill to a small house, surrounded by brown cattle.

'You keep out of this, you interfering old woman!' cried Thorgill. 'She's my daughter and I want her home to get her just punishment!'

'Goose poo to you, Thorgill!' retorted Grandmother. 'She's *my* daughter's daughter, and her poor mother would be turning in her grave if she knew how you and Gudrun treat her. It's quite clear the two of you don't really want her, so let me take her off your hands.'

'The cheek of you!' squawked Gudrun.

Grandmother glared at her. She turned to the fisherman. 'Just up there, my good man,' she said. And I'll find you a bar of silver straight away to thank you for your kindness.'

'Aw, if you're sure you can cope with her bad behaviour, you're welcome to her, you silly old woman!' spluttered Thorgill. 'Come on Gudrun, we'll go off and enjoy some peace and quiet.'

He turned his back and stomped off.

So Astrid went to live with Grandmother. By the time she'd got over her adventure, the first heavy snowfall of winter came, so she was forced to stay at home. But Grandmother promised Astrid lots of freedom once the spring melt came.

'I don't agree with keeping young girls tied to the weaving loom,' she said. 'One day you might be left with a farm to run yourself, Astrid, just like I was when your poor grandfather died, and we had no sons to take it over. So it's important you learn the ways of the world.'

25

On a sunny spring morning, when the lambs were gambolling and the wild apple trees were smothered in blossom, Captain Kvig's longship came sailing into the wide town fjord.

The ship rode low and sleek in the water: a sinuous black sea-serpent with a swan-shaped neck and a monstrous head. Along each of its sides thirty-two brightly painted shields stared unblinking, like evil eyes, and thirty-two massive oars rose and splashed in a steady rhythm. Its huge, blue-black sail billowed boldly in the wind.

Scores of people were crowded on the path above the beach to see the ship come in. They were all hoping for a glimpse of the pirates' loot: fishermen and busybody women, bent old gaffers, market traders and assorted children. Everyone was pushing and shoving. Astrid elbowed her way to the front, alongside a gang of excited little boys.

The longship steered in and the crew jumped out to haul it up the sand. Captain Kvig stood over them, shouting orders and brandishing his sword.

'Stand back, keep out of our way!' he yelled at the crowd.

A tall young man went to stand next to him. With a start, Astrid realised it was Bjarni. He was wearing a brand new tunic and trousers and a very smart fur hat. He looked really self-important. In his hand was the cursed sword.

The other pirates were filthy. They all crowded wearily up the beach, dragging empty bags. Captain Kvig got them to line up in front of a wall and shooed the crowd back. Then he swaggered up and down, making a great show as he held up armfuls of jewellery, sets of silver plates, precious glass vessels, bags of gold coins and so on, and dropped them into the pirates' bags. The crowd gawped and gasped and clapped.

Bjarni was the last to get his share, but it was by far the largest. Astrid was astonished to see how many gleaming things Captain Kvig dropped into his bag.

The pirates took their loot and went stomping off into the town centre, with a lot of crude talk about beer and women. Bjarni put his sword away, but he didn't look as if he intended to go with them, so Astrid ran up and grabbed his arm.

'Oh Bjarni,' she cried, 'you look fantastic. Where did you get those lovely clothes? And all that treasure the captain gave you! I'm so proud of you!'

Bjarni pushed her hand away self-consciously. 'Ya well, you know I can't keep any of the treasure,' he said. 'I've got to give it all to *him*, haven't I, to make sure he keeps his dirty hands off you.' He sighed. 'I suppose I'd better try and find him. You haven't seen him anywhere, have you?'

Astrid shook her head. 'Maybe he won't turn up this time, Bjarni? I mean, how would he know that you're back? Do you think you could...?'

Just then, a shifty looking man with a broken nose stepped out of the crowd and came up to them.

'Are you Bjarni the pirate lad?' he said.

'So what if I am?' said Bjarni.

'I've got a message for you,' said Broken Nose. 'It's from the girl's uncle.' He looked sideways at Astrid and sniffed. 'He says, you're to deliver the goods you owe him to Crow Beak Farm, and you know what'll happen if you don't.'

'Crow Beak Farm?' said Bjarni. 'Where's that? How do I get there?'

'It's in the mountains,' said Broken Nose. 'You'll have to catch a boat to the top of Needle Fjord, then climb the forest path to his house. Got it?'

Bjarni nodded, but Broken Nose had already disappeared into the crowd.

'I'd better do what he says,' said Bjarni. 'Do you know where I can find a ferry?'

Astrid pointed round the curve of the harbour to the far end.

'Do you want me to come with you?' she offered reluctantly.

'No,' said Bjarni quickly, 'I'll deal with this. You've got us in enough trouble already.'

Astrid flushed deep red. 'It wasn't me who got us into trouble,' she said.

'But you introduced me to Grim Gruesome,' said Bjarni.

'Well I didn't know it was him, did I? And I never told you to take the sword...'

'Well, you didn't exactly stop me either!'

'Don't blame me, Bjarni. Don't make an argument as soon as we're together again. You *wanted* to take it.'

'Ya, and I'm glad I did. It's a brilliant weapon! It's the type of sword I've always longed for!' He looked her in the eye. 'Or it would be...if I didn't have to give away all its winnings.'

The sword was hanging in its scabbard at his side. He put his hand to it and ran his fingers over the rune carvings. Astrid watched him. He didn't seem frightened of the runes any more: in fact, he seemed almost fond of them.

Astrid shuddered. Her conversation with the fortune teller flashed back into her mind: *you must seize the sword... fling it into the sea!* Here was an opportunity. She might not get another one.

Bjarni turned away from her and began to walk briskly round the harbour.

Astrid squeezed her Thor's-hammer pendant. She always wore it now. She ran after Bjarni and quickly caught him up. Bjarni ignored her.

The sword was bouncing against his leg with every step he took. Astrid walked on that side and gradually moved nearer, until it was close enough to touch.

Bjarni stared moodily ahead.

Astrid stretched her fingers out very gingerly, and brushed them against the hilt.

Bjarni didn't seem to notice.

They walked on. Astrid closed her fingers around the black, lambskin grip and pulled.

There was a soft scraping noise. The sword slid a little way up the scabbard. But it was so heavy! She strained to pull it further...

Suddenly Bjarni punched her hand, really hard!

She shrieked and let go. He grabbed her wrist and whirled round to face her.

'Dwarf spit!' he cried. 'What are you doing?'

'Don't swear at me, Bjarni!'

'Get your hands off my sword!'

'It's not *your* sword, Bjarni: it's still Grim Gruesome's, in case you've forgotten. I'm trying to help you Bjarni, I'm trying to free us from the curse. I've spoken to a fortune teller, and she told me to...'

'Don't you dare do anything to my beautiful Blood Drinker!'

'Blood Drinker?' said Astrid. 'Is that what you call it, Bjarni? Oh...that's *horrible.*'

'You're only a girl. What do you understand?'

Bjarni had turned red with fury. A little pool of froth was bubbling from the corner of his mouth. Astrid stood straight in front of him and tried to make him look at her. But his eyes wandered away from her gaze, back to the pirate ship. Kvig was still swaggering about in front of it and shouting. He saw Bjarni looking at him and waved his fist.

Bjarni pursed his lips. He pulled the sword clean from the scabbard - and pointed it at Astrid's chest.

Astrid screamed.

'Bjarni! Please...what are you doing? In mighty Thor's name, put it away! Don't play silly games. You're scaring me.'

'Good! Now you can see how much this sword - my Blood Drinker - means to me.'

'But it's turned you into a slave, Bjarni! You just said...'

'No it hasn't. It's turned me into Captain Kvig's right-hand man and earned me a load of respect from the rest of the crew. Just keep your hands off it, Astrid. Otherwise I'll...I'll slice them off!'

'Bjarni!' Astrid was crying. 'I'm your girlfriend! I love you...'

'Ya,' said Bjarni, 'and I love you too.' He groaned.

'You know I have to be a fighting man now, Astrid, so I can protect you. And I can't do that if you try and steal this sword.'

'But Bjarni, it's all because of the sword that Grim Gruesome's got us trapped. If we get rid of it - if we hurl it into the sea - that might free us from Grim Gruesome.'

'But don't you understand? Nothing in the world would make me want to get rid of the sword now. It's the best thing I've ever had in my life. It's made me into a hero.'

'You've always been a hero to me Bjarni,' said Astrid. 'But since you took the sword...oh Bjarni, you've changed. It's like...like the sword's the only thing that matters to you. It scares me. Can't you see, Bjarni? It's controlling you. It's all part of Grim Gruesome's trickery. He's used the sword to get you into his power, and in the end he'll hurt...'

'He never said he'd hurt *me*, Astrid. And so long as I keep bringing him treasure, he won't hurt you either. Isn't that enough to satisfy you? Now, I'll never get up to his place in the mountains with you clinging to me. Get out of my way!'

26

Bjarni slid the sword back into its scabbard. He slung his sack of treasure over his shoulders, staggering slightly under its bulk and weight. Then he turned his back on Astrid and strode off along the quayside.

At the far end, there was a row of small ferry boats waiting for passengers. Six or seven ferrymen were sheltering from the wind, leaning against a warehouse wall, sharing a grubby pot of beer. Bjarni went up to them.

'I need someone to take me to Crow Beak Farm,' he said.

The ferrymen all looked at each other and guffawed.

'Why ever would you want to go to that spook-infested dump, laddy?' asked a short, fat man. 'Don't you know, it's been deserted for over twenty years? There's nothing there but rats and dark-elves and ghosts.'

'It's right at the back of beyond,' said an old fellow, 'up the top of the gloomiest fjord in the kingdom.'

'Ya,' said the fat one, 'and to get to the old farmhouse you have to climb up a really steep, slippy path through thick forest. Anyway, it must be completely overgrown by now.'

'I...I have to meet someone there,' said Bjarni carefully. 'It's really urgent. Is there time to get up there before nightfall?'

The fat ferryman shook his head. 'Don't look at me to take you!'

The others all grunted in agreement.

'If you're dead set on going,' said the old one, 'you'd best row there yourself.'

'That's fine,' said Bjarni. 'Can one of you hire me out a boat?'

The others all pointed at the fat ferryman. He snorted sarcastically, then beckoned Bjarni closer. 'It won't be cheap, mind,' he said. 'You won't be able to get all the way there and back before tonight, so you'll have to pay me two days' rent. And I want a deposit on top of that - for the whole value of the boat - in case you get yourself into trouble up there and can't bring it back.'

'How much?' said Bjarni.

'I saw you come in with Kvig's pirate raiding crew. Your bag's bulging with loot, isn't it? Don't expect a bargain. I want thirty ounces of silver.'

'Dwarf spit!' cried Bjarni. 'That's robbery!'

The fat man shrugged. 'Suit yourself. It's all the same to me. The boat I'm willing to rent you is a good one and you'll get twenty-five back if you return it.'

Bjarni hesitated for a moment. Of course, he was supposed to give everything in his bag to Grim Gruesome. *But I won't be able to give him any of it unless I pay for a boat to his hideout*, he thought. *And with Kvig paying me double, there's much more than Grim expected. Anyway, he'll never know.*

'All right,' he said reluctantly.

The fat ferryman picked up a scale from the ground by the warehouse. While he was setting it up with weights, Bjarni fished about inside his treasure sack and pulled out two silver bars. The fat man weighed them. They were heavy, but not quite enough. Bjarni threw in a silver spoon. That made it a bit too much, so the fat man cut the spoon in half to get it right, and gave the spare half back to Bjarni. He dropped the silver into a big wooden box that he'd been sitting on, and locked it with an iron key. Then he led Bjarni to a boat and pointed out which way to go.

Bjarni jumped on board, pulling his treasure sack after him. He took up the oars and rowed quickly out of the harbour, north up the big fjord. It was very busy, with boats and ships coming and going in all directions, followed by streams of shrieking seagulls.

Bjarni followed the ferryman's directions. He turned right at the second side-fjord that he came to. Halfway along this, he turned left into Needle Fjord.

At once the sun disappeared. The fjord was as narrow and sharp as its name. Sheer cliffs towered on either side. Beyond them, snow-capped mountains rose into dark, swirling storm-clouds. The cliffs were bare and crusty, dotted with heaps of loose stones and stunted, half-dead trees. The water was completely still, black and bottomless.

There were no other boats here. There were no birds. The *swish-swish* of Bjarni's oars echoed between the silent cliffs.

As he rowed, the wind blew the storm-clouds across

to the fjord. They hung threateningly above him, then burst into a torrent of rain.

Bjarni was soaked through. Still he kept on rowing.

Needle Fjord grew narrower and narrower. At the very top there was just enough room to row into an old landing stage by some rocks. He threw the mooring rope round a wooden post. At once the post cracked and crumbled away.

'Arggh! Farting giantesses!' he roared.

Bjarni wrapped the rope round his arm, leaped ashore onto the rocks and heaved the boat clear of the water. Then he clambered up to where the forest started.

A small gap in the trees showed a winding, overgrown path.

The rain had stopped as suddenly as it had begun, but the trees were dripping. Bjarni took up the sack of treasure and drew out his sword. He started up the path, using the sword to slice through stray creepers and brambles.

It was so steep, he had to keep throwing the sack ahead so that he could use his hands to haul himself up. He climbed over huge boulders. He almost lost his footing on a long stretch of unmelted ice. He leaped over enormous fallen tree trunks. He turned sharply round a bend.

'What the...?' he yelled in surprise.

For the place wasn't deserted after all. A man was squatting in the middle of the path!

He was big and fat. He wore a shabby, rain-spattered cloak and a battered hat with an unusually wide brim. The hat cast a deep shadow over his face. But Bjarni could see that his beard was dark and ragged, and a filthy bandage was wrapped around his eyes.

'Who's there?' called the man in an ugly, rasping voice. 'What do you want?' He held out his hands blindly. They were covered by mangy fur gloves. 'Thor's thunderballs! You'd better have something good enough to give a starving beggar. Otherwise I'll kick you straight back down the mountain!'

27

Astrid sat down on the harbour wall, choking back the tears. *I knew he'd never let me throw the sword in the sea,* she thought. *I've failed again. I'm useless!*

She watched Bjarni going across to the ferries and arguing with the men. She saw the fat ferryman leading him to the rowing boat. She saw Bjarni reach into the sack to pay him.

He can't give him Grim Gruesome's treasure! she thought. *Supposing he finds out? Oh Thor save me! He'll start doing all those evil things!*

She stared after Bjarni's boat, chewing her fingernails in an agony of worry. Slowly Bjarni rowed down the fjord and out of sight.

Should I go after him? Should I give Grim Gruesome some of my own valuables to make up for what Bjarni's taken out? Her stomach clenched and churned at the thought.

She stroked her four silver rings across her cheek. She fingered the gleaming gold neckband she always wore, and her jangling silver bracelets.

I can't! Mother gave them to me when she was dying - it's all I've got left of her - she said I should keep them for ever. And yet...

Suddenly she felt very cold. She remembered the fateful day at the harbour, when Bjarni had asked her to lend him some of her jewellery to buy a sword. *It was Grim Gruesome who said I shouldn't,* she thought. *Otherwise I might have done - and he wouldn't have been able to trap us!*

The fortune teller's words came nagging into her mind: *'...go back to him of your own free will...give him something that you cannot bear to give.'*

She shuddered and got up with a sigh. *This is my last chance. I'll have to!*

She pulled the walrus-ivory comb from from her belt and tidied up her hair, then smoothed down her dress.

But he's not having my Thor's-hammer. I need it.

She clasped the hammer in her fist and said a silent

prayer to it. Then she unclipped its chain and hid it in her purse.

She pinched her cheeks to make them look rosy and fixed her face into a false smile. At last she was ready. She walked across to the ferries.

'Please, could someone take me up the fjord after that boy who just hired a boat?' she said.

At first all the men just laughed at her:

'What's a nice girl like you doing, running after a dirty pirate lad?'

'Watch out girlie, he'll be up to mischief if you catch him up!'

'Crow Beak Farm's an evil place - keep away from it, sweetheart!'

But Astrid was good at getting round people. Simply being rich and pretty was usually enough. She giggled, simpered and fluttered her eyelashes. Then she pulled off one of her rings and offered it in payment.

The ferrymen all started nudging each other and the youngest one turned bright red.

'Aw, come on then,' he said, 'I'll take you.'

28

The blind beggar stood up unsteadily and came towards Bjarni. He sniffed the air like a dog and his bullying manner changed to a whine:

'You've got to help me! They beat me up and stole everything, then left me in this wilderness for dead. I haven't eaten anything for days!'

'I feel sorry for you,' said Bjarni, 'but I haven't got anything to eat. I haven't eaten myself all day.'

He tried to skirt round the beggar. But although he was blind and in a terrible state, the beggar was quick. Suddenly he stuck out his leg. Bjarni couldn't stop himself: he tripped over it and went sprawling onto the ground. The sack fell from his hand with a loud clatter.

'Aha!' cried the beggar, 'I knew it! You've got

loads of treasure in there. Give me some! Reckon I could buy a whole roast cow with that lot. Come on, don't be mean, share it. Remember what Odin said: *The brave and generous have the best lives.* '

'Treasure won't be any use to you here,' said Bjarni. 'There's nowhere to buy food.' He grabbed the sack and held onto it tightly. 'Anyway, it's not mine, so I can't give any away.'

'Whose is it then, eh?' said the beggar. 'So you're a thief are you, as well as a mangy piece of scum?'

'Get out of my way!' cried Bjarni.

But instead, the beggar began to dance about in front of him, blocking the narrow path. He punched his fists into the empty air and kicked out in all directions.

Bjarni put the sack down again, drew the cursed sword...and went for him!

He didn't want to kill the beggar, so he struck him hard on the legs. But the blade bounced off as if the wretch's boots were made of iron. Bjarni swore, and this time went shamelessly for the beggar's chest.

But the beggar stood dead still, unseeing, unflinching and grinning. Bjarni was completely unnerved. His arm went limp, and he missed his target.

147

He couldn't believe it. The sword had never let him down before. *What ever's wrong with it?* he thought. He broke out in a cold sweat. 'Let me pass!' he cried.

'Not unless you give me some of that treasure!'

'Odin's eye socket!' swore Bjarni. He opened his sack and started to fish about in it, glancing around guiltily.

'Hurry up, hurry up!' the beggar hissed.

Bjarni pulled out a gold arm-band. It was broken and scratched, hardly worth worrying about. 'Here, you can have this,' he said. 'Now let me get on!'

He dropped the arm-band into the beggar's outstretched hand. The mangy glove closed around it and the beggar gave an ugly chuckle. Then he turned about and pushed his way noisily into the thick tangle of trees and brambles that bordered the path.

Bjarni stared after him for a moment, wondering where he'd gone. Then he gave a sigh of relief and went back to his climb.

It took ages. The sky grew dark with storm clouds again and a wind came whistling down the mountain. But at last he came to a large, level ridge.

The forest had been cleared away from it to form a rough field, covered in dead brown grass and surrounded by a broken wooden fence. An icy stream rushed down over the stones on the far edge. A small wooden farmhouse stood in the shelter of the rock face.

The door of the house was half open.

Bjarni paused to get his breath back, then set out across the field. It was sodden and boggy from the rain and littered with piles of horse dung, but there was no sign of any animal. He reached the door and peered inside.

The house was in darkness. The fire was cold. No lamps were burning.

But through the shadows, he saw something moving.

29

Bjarni's eyes adjusted to the gloom. He made out a small room. There were rough benches running along the sides, but no furniture. A big weaving loom stood against the back wall. A stout woman sat on a stool, bent towards it, working at it in the darkness.

'Excuse me,' Bjarni called out softly.

The loom shuttle went *clickety-clack, clickety-clack.* The woman didn't turn round. She didn't stop working. But after a few moments, she called back in a hoarse voice:

'Who are you? What do you want?'

'I...I'm looking for someone,' said Bjarni. 'This is Crow Beak Farm, isn't it? I was told to meet him here.'

'There's no one here but me,' she answered.

Clickety-clack. Clickety-clack. Clickety-clack.

'It's lonely up here on the mountain,' the woman said suddenly. 'It gets very cold at night. I suppose you'll be wanting to stay here, eh?' She gave a cackle of laughter. 'Well, come in, boy, come in.'

Bjarni stepped inside.

'Make yourself useful,' she said. 'Light the fire.'

Bjarni took the fire-making kit that hung from his belt, struck a flame and put it to some kindling sticks in the fire-pit. Soon the logs flared alight.

Now he could see the woman a little more clearly. She was unusually tall as well as stout. She wore a dark dress and her head and shoulders were wrapped in a vast black shawl. She kept her back to him, and called out again:

'If you want something to eat, and a blanket to sleep under, you realise you'll have to pay me.'

Bjarni sighed. What could he do? Reluctantly he dumped his sack on one of the wall-benches and rummaged inside it. He pulled out a small silver cup, put it back guiltily, then pulled it out again.

'Would this be enough, ma'am?'

'Bring it over. Let's have a look.'

He carried the bowl across to the loom. Still the woman didn't turn round. Instead she held out her left hand.

'Give it to me.'

Bjarni made to place the bowl in her hand...and stopped.

In the flickering firelight, he could see that the woman had only four fingers. They were big and masculine. Instead of the little finger there was a blackened stump.

Very slowly, the woman turned round. Her shawl hung deeply over her face; but under it, Bjarni glimpsed a familiar pattern of hollows and shadows. And a thick, black beard.

'Grim?' he whispered.

'Welcome, Bjarni,' said Grim Gruesome. He stood up and threw off the woman's shawl with a flourish. Underneath was his dark, hooded cloak.

'You're very eager to give away my treasure, aren't you?,' he said. 'Even though I commanded you to bring all of it to me.' His voice grew low and menacing. '*All* of it, Bjarni! How dare you go round handing out shares to any beggar or old woman who asks for it! Did you really think you could get away with it?'

'I...I didn't...'

'I was there,' said Grim. 'I saw you, Bjarni. *I* was

the beggar, you fool! Just as I was the old woman you thought you saw just now. Both times, you were going to cheat me, Bjarni!'

'No sir! I...'

'I warned you not to disobey me. You know very well what the consequences are.'

'But...but...' Bjarni stammered, 'Captain Kvig gave me much more treasure than you expected, sir, so I thought...Anyway, I only handed over the bowl because I realised it was you, sir...I mean, at first I thought I saw a woman at the weaving loom...but I guessed almost straight away...'

'Liar!'

'Honestly, I...'

'And what about that boat you hired to bring you here up the Needle Fjord? How much of my silver did you pay to the wretch who rented it to you?'

'I didn't...I didn't actually *pay* anything, sir...I just gave him a deposit. He said, when I take the boat back, he'll repay the silver. So next time I see you sir, I promise I'll give it back to you...'

Bjarni could feel Grim's eyes boring through him. He backed away and tried to hide his face. Grim stepped after him, hands outstretched. His nine long, hairy fingers clawed at the air. The blackened stump twitched with a life of its own.

'You like to pretend you're a man now, don't you, tagging along with those pirates?' he mocked. 'But I only have to blink and you're cringing like a cornered mouse. You're like every child I've ever met - pathetic and despicable!'

The words tore at Bjarni's pride. *I can't let him put me down like that,* he thought. *He doesn't realise I'm Kvig's second-in-command. I've got to stand up to him!*

He straightened up and drew the cursed sword from its scabbard.

'This is my Blood Drinker now,' he said. 'I can beat everyone with it - even you!'

'But Bjarni,' said Grim, 'because you cheated me, you've got to give the sword back to me.'

Bjarni shook his head and tightened his grip, ready to strike.

'GIVE IT TO ME!' Grim roared. His outstretched hands opened and closed like wolf jaws.

Bjarni's breath came in heavy, desperate gasps. His fingers turned slippery with sweat.

Grim Gruesome thumped his deformed hand hard onto Bjarni's wrist. Bjarni gave a roar of pain. The cursed sword slid from his hand onto the floor.

'No!' shrieked Bjarni, 'NO!' Tears of rage and despair blurred his eyes. He lunged forward and tried to grab it back.

But Grim was faster. He swooped on the sword like a starving bird of prey, seized it and dangled it tantalisingly in front of Bjarni's face.

Bjarni tried desperately to grab it. The blade danced just beyond his reach, stabbing and scratching at his fingers.

'You are nothing without this sword, Bjarni!' Grim taunted him. 'You are feebler than a worm, less than a grain of dust.'

He gave a screech of unearthly laughter. Then he whirled round...

And flung the cursed sword into the fire!

30

The yellow flames leaped up around the sword like greedy snake tongues.

'It will melt,' said Grim. 'It will dissolve into a lump of useless metal. You will never hold the sword again. You will never see it again. And all the strength you thought you had will dissolve away with it.'

'Sir, please...I beg you!'

'It was your choice to break our bargain, Bjarni,' said Grim.

'I didn't break it! You've got to believe me!'

'...And so, your choice to see your little lovebird - that simpering fool of a girl Astrid - suffer.' Grim Gruesome snorted with laughter. 'Don't worry, Bjarni, it was the right choice. Because as a reward, you can help me torment her.'

'No!' cried Bjarni. He tried his utmost to keep his voice manly and steady. But to his shame, the words jerked out in a squeaky gulp. 'I'll never hurt Astrid. And I won't let you either, Grim...I'll kill you!'

'You couldn't even kill a maggot without the cursed sword. Besides, Bjarni: it's impossible to kill me.'

Grim Gruesome stood towering over Bjarni. His hidden gaze bored into him. His putrid smell of rotting flesh wafted up Bjarni's nostrils.

Bjarni backed away towards the door. He couldn't take his eyes off the cursed sword, shimmering in the golden heat of the fire.

'I'm ravenously hungry, Bjarni,' said Grim Gruesome. 'It's years since I last tasted a child's screams. And it'll add delicious spice to have you squirming with horror beside me, as I destroy your beloved girlfriend.'

Bjarni felt he would suffocate from Grim's stench. He felt a throbbing in his head.

But no, it wasn't his head. It was outside, an ominous, steady banging.

Was it the wind battering loose panels on the crumbling farmhouse walls? Was it rain drumming on the old turf roof? No, it was a rapping at the door.

Bjarni had his back to it. He didn't see it slowly open.

Grim Gruesome's deep laugh quivered round the room. He waggled his finger stump, then suddenly pointed at something behind Bjarni's back.

Bjarni spun round...

And saw Astrid standing in the doorway.

31

Astrid's climb through the rain and the lonely forest had left her shattered. She was flushed and sweating. Her hair had come loose from its braids and ribbons. It hung over her shoulders in a wet, dishevelled mess, gleaming like white-gold in the firelight. Her delicate shoes were in shreds, and her feet were bare and bleeding.

Grim Gruesome held her in his faceless, penetrating gaze. The blood drained from her face. Then she jerked her eyes away from him.

'Bjarni!' she gasped, 'I - I found something. You must have dropped it on your way up here.'

She reached under her sopping cloak and pulled out the broken gold arm-ring that Bjarni had given to the blind beggar.

Bjarni stared at her in bewilderment.

'You're too late, Astrid,' rasped Grim Gruesome. 'Bjarni's already broken our bargain by stealing some of my treasure.'

'He didn't steal it!' cried Astrid. 'He just lost it... Look, I've brought it straight to you sir, here!'

She thrust the arm-ring at Grim. He hurled it to the floor.

'And another thing,' said Astrid breathlessly, 'in case you're angry that he had to pay for a boat to get here...' She began to unclip her gold neck-band and pull off her bracelets and rings, one by one. 'These are really valuable, sir, they were my mother's, they're worth a huge weight of silver. You can have them, sir, to make up for...'

She held them out, looking at Grim Gruesome hopefully.

He snatched them from her, spat on them and dropped them.

'What a cowardly maggot you are, Bjarni!' he hissed. 'Letting a girl - a *girl* of all creatures - try and cover up your mistakes! Oh Astrid, to think that you once tried to convince me that he was a hero. Can't you see? He's really just a piece of rubbish, like your father said. He can't be bothered to protect you any more. In fact, he's going to help me torture you.'

'Bjarni?' cried Astrid. 'I don't believe this! You...'

'Oh, don't go looking to him for any comfort,' sneered Grim. 'He left a clear trail for you to follow, didn't he, straight into my den!'

He made a slurping noise inside his hood, as if he were licking his lips. Then he held up his left hand.

The rotting finger-stump was just a breath away from Astrid's face. Slowly Grim began to move it back and forth, back and forth. It wriggled like a stunted black slug, oozing yellow pus.

Astrid screwed up her eyes.

Grim forced them open with his other hand.

'There is no hiding from me, Astrid,' he said softly. 'I have tentacles like a sea monster. They are invisible, but they are already worming their way into your heart. They are sinking into the secret corners of your mind, gripping you, sucking out your last grains of happiness. There is darkness creeping through your blood.' He whipped his finger away and bent the murky pool of his head to her. 'But of course, you've seen it already, Astrid...*haven't you?!*'

Astrid's mind whirled back to all the

dream-haunted nights she had spent tossing and turning, since Bjarni took the cursed sword.

'Y... ya,' she whispered.

'Then tremble, you wretched child,' said Grim. 'For from now on, you will never sleep again!'

Astrid was deathly white. She clenched her fists. She bit her upper lip so hard it began to bleed.

'B...bu...but you...you've got no right!' she whispered. Her mouth opened and closed like a fish as she tried to fight Grim's spells and form the words. 'I told you, Bjarni didn't...he d...didn't steal anything. He...'

'He betrayed you, Astrid,' said Grim.

Suddenly he grabbed her arms. With a great roar, he lifted her right up and began to spin her, round and round. High over the fire he swung her - then head-over-heels, down and round into dark, spider-ridden corners.

Astrid began to scream hysterically. But Bjarni saw his chance!

He leaped to the fire. The cursed sword glowed in the middle of the flames.

Behind him Grim had pushed Astrid to the floor. He was hissing foul, terrifying spells at her.

Bjarni seized a heavy iron poker that lay under a pile of spare logs at the side of the hearth. He jabbed it into the flames and used it to push the sword to the side of the fire-pit.

The sword tumbled over the edge to the floor. It was still whole. But it was white-hot - too hot to touch.

In the shadows behind him, Grim raged and Astrid sobbed.

Bjarni tore off his rain-sodden tunic. He scrunched it up and wound it round his right hand like a bandage, as a shield from the heat. He grabbed the scorching hilt of the sword...

SSSsssss! The wet cloth sent up a cloud of steam and the heat seared through it to Bjarni's hand. He dropped it quickly. The cloth unwound itself, leaving the hilt exposed.

Bjarni stared at it in disbelief.

The rune letters and Lappish marks had all burnt away. The black iron guard was blank. The curse had vanished!

32

At that moment, Grim whirled round.

'I see you, Bjarni!' he roared.

He kicked Astrid into a corner. Then he drew out an ancient, blood-stained sword of his own and leaped at Bjarni.

Bjarni jumped away and snatched up the cursed sword from the floor. At first he winced, because it was still searing hot. But almost at once the sword's familiar lightening power surged through his veins. He stood tall, hurled himself at Grim Gruesome - and they began to fight!

Their swords clashed and clinked. Their feet pounded around the hard mud floor. Grim Gruesome loomed over Bjarni like a monstrous troll. His dark cloak was a span of crow-wings. In the shadows of his hood, his eyes gleamed like glowing coals, heavy with the promise of death.

All the pirate battles Bjarni had ever fought - all those battles he had won - flashed through his mind and gave him strength. In the red firelight, he struck his sword fearlessly and daringly back against Grim's sword - like this! - like that!

They staggered round the fire-pit. They backed up against the walls. They stumbled over Astrid, who lay moaning in a corner by the door. They leaped and ducked. Their swords clanged and smashed together.

Bjarni stopped for an instant to get his breath. Then he gritted his teeth, lurched forward and shoved the cursed sword hard into the folds of Grim's cloak, aiming for his heart...

But Grim was faster, Grim was stronger.

Before the cursed sword could even graze him, Grim grabbed the blade with his bare hands and shoved it hard away. Bjarni teetered and almost lost his balance. Grim began to rain sword blows onto him.

There was blood everywhere. Bjarni's head swam and blackness engulfed him. The floor came up towards him...

I've failed, he thought. *After all this, Grim's beaten me.*

'You coward, Bjarni!' Grim Gruesome mocked. 'You weakling! Look at him, Astrid, drowning in his own shame.'

Bjarni was on fire with pain. His legs began to buckle.

'No, Bjarni!' Astrid screamed at him. 'Fight him! You've got to keep going.'

He blinked his eyes open, and saw her in the corner, cowering in the dim firelight.

She actually dared come after me, he thought. *Right up the mountain! Through the forest! She knew Grim Gruesome was here, she knew he'd get her. I can't give up on her now!*

He took a gasp of air, licked the trickling blood from his cheek and tightened his grip on the cursed sword. He stepped back and twisted round, ducking Grim Gruesome's blows, and darted past the villain, round to the far side of the fire-pit.

'You haven't beaten me yet!' he panted. 'Even if I die fighting you, I'll get Astrid free of you first!'

Grim gave a belch of laughter. He strode round the left side of the fire-pit towards Bjarni, brandishing his bloodied sword.

At once Bjarni darted to the right.

Grim spun round and came after him that way.

Bjarni doubled back to the first side.

Grim stopped and flung his cloak back over his shoulders. In the flickering firelight he looked massive, iron hard, bulging with muscles. He stepped back to the wall, took a run at the fire-pit - and sprang from the floor!

Bjarni glanced wildly round. His wet tunic was still lying where he'd dropped it. He darted down, grabbed it and hurled it hard at Grim's head.

Grim was in mid-air, leaping over the flames. *Thwack!* The wet shirt thumped under his hood, into the darkness of his eyes.

'GUTS AND PUS!' he roared.

He lurched over to the side...and tumbled plunging into the flames.

'YAARCCHHHH!'

'He's burning!' Astrid screamed.

Grim Gruesome righted himself and came charging from the fire-pit, waving his arms. But already the flames were engulfing him.

Astrid had managed to stagger to her feet. 'Quickly!' she yelled to Bjarni.

Grim Gruesome was a towering pillar of fire and

smoke, teetering towards them.

'Get out!' Astrid screamed. 'Run!'

She turned to the door and pulled at the handle. It burst open suddenly, letting in the cold night wind and another torrent of rain. She stumbled outside...

Almost at once, Bjarni was beside her. He slammed the door shut behind them. He came dragging out his hard-won sack of treasure - and still clasping the cursed sword.

33

Night had fallen. There was no moon. There were no stars. But somehow Bjarni and Astrid stumbled across the sloping, dead-grass meadow and found the overgrown path. Slowly but surely, they climbed down the mountain.

Owls hooted and screeched. Somewhere, high up on the peaks, a horse whinnied eerily.

Neither Bjarni nor Astrid spoke. They hardly knew what they were doing.

The rain pelted down on them. Stones slithered and tumbled under their aching feet. Elf shadows darted through the darkness. Distant wolves howled on the moaning wind.

But they reached the bottom safely at last.

Dawn was coming up behind the mountains to the

east. There was just enough light to see the water's edge and the rocks by the landing stage. The fat ferryman's boat was still where Bjarni had left it. He helped Astrid into it and tossed the sword - the once-cursed sword - under the rowing bench. Then he pushed the boat down into the water and rowed her out into the black waters of Needle Fjord.

By the time they reached the town harbour, they were grinning at each other. And the spring day was full of sunshine.

34

A few hours later, Astrid and Bjarni were sitting side by side in Grandmother's farmhouse, wrapped in warm blankets, and sharing a delicious stewed goose.

'I can't believe you two have been tangled up with Grim Gruesome!' cried Grandmother. 'Astrid, my poor princess! Why ever didn't you tell me?'

'I tried to, Grandmother, but you wouldn't listen.'

'Of course I would have listened. I would have called up some men to drive the brute away. But to think: you actually managed to escape him! That's supposed to be impossible!'

She carved them both another huge helping of goose.

'Just wait until everyone hears about how you fought him off, Bjarni...'

'And *destroyed* him, Grandmother!' said Astrid.

'Ya, princess, I know, I know. The poets will make you into a famous hero, Bjarni. Your name will be carved on rune-stones. People will have pictures of you fighting Grim Gruesome embroidered into tapestries and carved on their doors!'

Astrid clutched Bjarni's hand and squealed with pride. But Bjarni looked embarrassed. He stood up awkwardly.

'Thank you for the meal, ma'am,' he said. 'Um, I'm sorry, I can't stay any longer. I've got to get back to my ship. We're sailing again tomorrow and Kvig gets furious if anyone keeps him waiting.'

'Oh no, Bjarni,' cried Astrid, 'you're not going away again? Please don't! You don't need to, now Grim's finished and the curse has burnt away. And you've already got a whole sack of treasure.'

'But it isn't enough to pay that huge bride-price your father wants for you,' said Bjarni. 'Um...that's if you still want to marry me?'

Astrid turned bright red. 'Of course I do,' she said. 'But...surely you could earn some more silver without going back to those horrible pirates? I hate all that stealing and killing. Grandmother, tell him not to!'

'Well,' said Grandmother carefully, 'you know princess, treasure gathering and fighting and all the rest is *men's* business - we women mustn't interfere. Just because Grim Gruesome led Bjarni into it, doesn't mean it's not respectable.'

'But I've seen the other pirates on Bjarni's ship,' said Astrid. 'They're all horrible ruffians!'

'They might not be as bad as they seem,' said Grandmother. 'Didn't I ever tell you? My own father used to do a bit of pirating every spring.'

Astrid's mouth dropped open. 'No!' she said.

'It's true,' said Grandmother. 'And of course, Norway wouldn't be so rich and mighty if great King Harald Fairhair hadn't used pirates to fill the kingdom's treasure chests. You should be proud that Bjarni's following such a bold tradition.'

Bjarni nodded gratefully at Grandmother.

'Ya,' he said, 'and it's not just to pay the bride-price. Because your father's right on one thing, Astrid: a well-bred girl like you can't marry a poor servant. So I'm going to keep gathering treasure until I've got enough to take you abroad - to one of the new countries. We'll go to England or Iceland, and buy a farm of our own out there.'

'A farm of our own?' cried Astrid. 'Oh Bjarni!'

Bjarni grinned sheepishly. He picked up the sack of treasure he'd carried all the way up and down the mountain and slung it over his shoulder. Then he slipped out of the door.

Astrid ran after him. 'Where are you taking all that stuff now, Bjarni?'

'I'm going to bury it on the way back to town,' he said. 'Somewhere secret where no one can steal it. Ya, I know, that's just like your father, Astrid - but I've got to practise how to be rich. When I come back in a few months, I should have a whole load more to add to it.'

He pulled out the once-cursed sword and tapped the hilt teasingly on her nose. Grandmother beamed at them indulgently, then went back inside, closing the door firmly.

So Bjarni seized his chance as he always did. He pulled Astrid close, and for the first time in ages he kissed her.

Then they said goodbye and Bjarni set off down the road to town. And who should he meet on the way? None other than Gudrun and Thorgill.

They were on their way to Grandmother's house. Thorgill wanted to make sure that she was keeping

Astrid under proper control. It was lucky he didn't know about her hair raising adventures!

When they saw Bjarni coming along, they stopped as if they couldn't believe their eyes. Gudrun muttered some very rude and nasty words. Thorgill turned purple and yelled at the top of his voice:

'You boy! I never thought I'd see your weasly face again. How dare you come sneaking back round here. If you're harassing my daughter again, I'll...I'll...'

'Have him outlawed!' cried Gudrun.

'That's too much palaver for a worm like him,' said Thorgill. 'I'd rather deal with him quickly myself.'

He drew his sword and went for Bjarni.

But to his astonishment, Bjarni pulled out a sword of his own - a truly magnificent sword, one that must have been worth a fortune! As they drew closer, he realised, with another start, that Bjarni had grown much taller and his shoulders were broader; he was even sprouting the first wisps of a beard.

He was even more astonished at Bjarni's fighting skills. It only took a few quick blows for Bjarni to send Thorgill sprawling onto the ground.

Bjarni stood looking down at him. What was the right thing to do? This was Astrid's father, after all.

Should he apologise? But he couldn't bring himself to, not after the way Thorgill had treated him.

So he said cockily, 'I'm as good as you now, sir! I'm a pirate captain's second-in-command. No one can beat me in a sword fight.' Then he felt a bit ashamed, so he put his sword away. 'But...um, I don't mind forgetting all those bad things you did to me.'

'Just listen to his cheek!' scolded Gudrun.

Bjarni ignored her. He said, 'Shall we make peace, sir?' and held out his hand.

Thorgill struggled to his feet and spat at it.

Bjarni shrugged. Then, whistling cheerfully, he went strutting off down the road towards town.

Thorgill stared after him, shaking his fist. 'You rat!' he cursed. 'You lump of pig turd! I'll get even with you...!'

Grandmother came rushing out.

'Oh, stop your prattling,' she snapped. 'Just you wait until you hear what we've got to tell you about that lad, Thorgill. You'll be frothing at the mouth to get Astrid married to him. You've already seen what a good swordsman he is, eh? Well he's also doing really well for himself, building up a huge store of his own treasure. And even more impressive: he's just rescued our Astrid from the clutches of Grim Gruesome!'

'*Grim Gruesome!?*' cried Thorgill.

'Ya!' said Grandmother. 'And he's burnt the villain to death!'

35

And that's almost the end of their story.

Over the next few years, Bjarni and his amazing sword won piles and piles more treasure. By the time he and Astrid turned sixteen, he was seriously rich. With all that treasure around, Thorgill couldn't help but be impressed. In the end he agreed to free Astrid from her betrothal to his old friend, and let her marry Bjarni instead.

Their wedding was the best and biggest feast ever held at Thorgill's farm - and that's saying something!

Then Bjarni left Kvig and the pirates' ship. He and Astrid sailed to England together and bought a big farm in a green valley. Astrid made sure they took her beloved Grandmother too. Everything worked out really well for them.

But unfortunately, it wasn't the end of Grim Gruesome after all. Somehow the gristly villain survived the fire.

How did he do it? How did he stay alive when he should have been burnt black as cinders? And how did he escape down the mountain?

Nobody knew for sure. Some people said he worked spells to do it. Others reckoned it was all due to Haski.

They said the wily horse was grazing on the high peaks when he heard Grim below, screaming with pain. They said he must have run down on the storm to Crow Beak Farm, forced the door open and lain beside Grim to heal him with his mysterious horse-warmth.

Nine nights later, some fishermen were out catching lobsters near the mouth of Needle Fjord. They saw a strange boat emerge from it, with no sail and no-one rowing it. As it drifted past them on the current, they made out a huge man in a deep-hooded cloak hunched inside it. Beside him stood a black horse with a silver mane.

The fishermen called out, but the hooded man didn't answer. The boat went on, slowly, silently, towards some lonely islands and vanished into the mist.

After that, dark rumours spread. They told how the skin on Grim's right arm had turned into a permanent, red mess of blistery burns, and that he relished the pain of them. For this pain was like a new weapon for him: it sharpened his appetite for tormenting children.

But if you want to know how he used it, you'll have to wait. Because that's another grim and gruesome story!

'Wolf-guts! Whale-doom! This I swear:
I'll stalk vile children everywhere.
I'll snatch and spike them in my snare
and boil their bones in dark despair!'

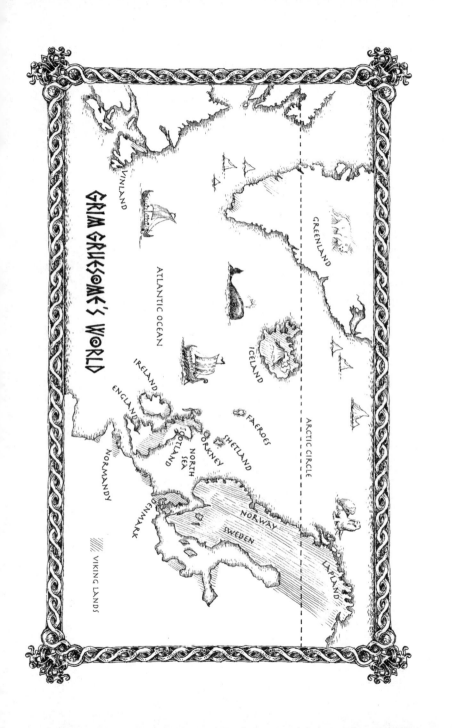

GRIM GRUESOME
VIKING VILLAIN

THE QUEEN'S POISON

ISBN: 978-0-9537454-4-9

The child-hating villain Grim Gruesome is on his way
to the Viking town of Jorvik! Dalla and her brothers
Aki and Frodi are terrified. Should the three children
trust the fierce 'berserk' warrior who offers them
protection? Or seek help from the Queen of Jorvik –
even though everyone says she's a witch?

Shape-shifting, riddles, sword fights and dramatic
chases through the narrow streets of a real Viking town
will sweep you along in another immensely readable,
fast moving historical thriller!

Look out
for the third Grim Gruesome book,

TROLLS' TREASURE

coming early in 2010.

It's another thrilling adventure
set in a sea-washed Viking island realm
and crammed with
mystery,
treasure and
sword-fights!

Have you visited
the Grim Gruesome website yet?

go to:

www.grimgruesome.com

★ Find out more about the Grim Gruesome books!
★ Download colourful bookmark designs!
★ Play the Grim Gruesome board game!
★ Learn interesting facts about the Viking Age!
★ Meet author Rosalind Kerven!

SOME OTHER BOOKS

by

ROSALIND KERVEN

Who Ever Heard of a Vegetarian Fox?

The Sea is Singing

Sorcery and Gold

Wild!

Mysteries of the Seals

The Reindeer and the Drum

King Arthur

English Fairy Tales and Legends

Earth Magic, Sky Magic

In the Court of the Jade Emperor

The Rain Forest Storybook

The Giant King: Looking at Norse Myths

The Fairy Spotter's Handbook

Aladdin and other Tales from the Arabian Nights

The Secret World of Magic

The Enchanted Forest

The Mythical Quest